Had the roaring decreased? She wasn't sure.

"How you doing?" he asked.

She could hear him now. He wasn't shouting.

"I don't want to die," she whispered. The words came as a surprise to her. Yesterday there was nothing she wanted to do. Nowhere she wanted to go. And now she just wanted to see the sky again. Dive into cold water. Inhale the scent of peonies.

"We're both going to live." He brushed his cheek against hers. "I'll keep you safe, Meadow. It won't get you."

She closed her eyes and tried to control the ball of pain that wanted to escape her throat as a sob. She failed. Here she had thought there was only a thin veil of foil between her and the fire. But it wasn't so. Dylan stood between her and the flames. He protected her with his body and his promise and she loved him for it.

FIREWOLF

—

JENNA KERNAN

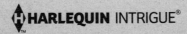
HARLEQUIN INTRIGUE®

This book is dedicated to hotshots with special consideration
to the Granite Mountain Hotshots and their families.

ISBN-13: 978-1-335-72099-3

Firewolf

Copyright © 2017 by Jeannette H. Monaco

Recycling programs
for this product may
not exist in your area.

Printed in U.S.A.

Jenna Kernan has penned over two dozen novels and has received two RITA® Award nominations. Jenna is every bit as adventurous as her heroines. Her hobbies include recreational gold prospecting, scuba diving and gem hunting. Jenna grew up in the Catskills and currently lives in the Hudson Valley of New York State with her husband. Follow Jenna on Twitter, @jennakernan, on Facebook or at jennakernan.com.

Books by Jenna Kernan

Harlequin Intrigue

Apache Protectors: Tribal Thunder

Turquoise Guardian
Eagle Warrior
Firewolf

Apache Protectors

Shadow Wolf
Hunter Moon
Tribal Law
Native Born

Harlequin Historical

Gold Rush Groom
The Texas Ranger's Daughter
Wild West Christmas
A Family for the Rancher
Running Wolf

Harlequin Nocturne

Dream Stalker
Ghost Stalker
Soul Whisperer
Beauty's Beast
The Vampire's Wolf
The Shifter's Choice

Visit the Author Profile page at Harlequin.com for more titles.

CAST OF CHARACTERS

Dylan Tehauno—A Turquoise Warrior, former US marine and hotshot with a sterling reputation. Dylan is every mother's dream son-in-law.

Meadow Wrangler—Tabloid socialite with a reputation that is all bad. Daughter of Theron and Lupe Wrangler.

Theron Wrangler—A documentary filmmaker, nationally recognized environmentalist, possible member of the eco-extremist group known as BEAR and Meadow's father.

Lupe Wrangler—A wealthy oil heiress, fund-raiser for her husband's causes and Meadow's judgmental mother.

Jack Bear Den—A detective with the tribal police and a Turquoise Guardian.

Joe Rhodes—Theron Wrangler's sound production man and a longtime colleague.

Katrina Wrangler—One of Meadow's older sisters who has helped Meadow out of scrapes in the past.

Kenshaw Little Falcon—The head of the Turquoise Guardians medicine society, his tribe's medicine man and a spiritual leader with strong ties to community, tradition and the land as well as possible ties to the eco-extremist group known as BEAR.

Luke Forrest—Black Mountain Apache and FBI agent in charge of investigating the Lilac Mine Slaying.

Cheney Williams—Production partner of Theron Wrangler and an attorney specializing in environmental law. Cheney is a former army ranger and friend of Kenshaw Little Falcon.

Chapter One

Dylan Tehauno would not have stopped for the woman if she had not been standing in the road. Her convertible was parked beside her, a black Audi of all things, impractical as her attire. It was impossible that she did not hear him crunching over the gravel road. Yet she continued to stare in the opposite direction, presenting him with a very tempting view of her backside and long bare legs.

Killer curves, he thought, as dangerous as the switchbacks between him and his destination on the mountain's ridgeline. Her pale skin had tanned to the color of wild honey. The Anglo woman wore no hat, and only a fool went out without one in the Arizona sun at midday in July. He let his gaze caress her curves again as she sidestepped and he glimpsed what he had not seen beyond that round rump. She was bent over a small tripod that had spindly black spider legs. Each leg was braced with a sandbag. On the pinnacle sat one of those little fist-sized mobile video cameras.

Her convertible blocked the right lane and her camera sat on the left. There was just no way around her as the graded gravel road dropped off on each side to thick scrub brush and piñon pine. It was a long way from his reservation in Turquoise Canyon to Flagstaff, not in miles, but in everything else that mattered. There were some pines down here, piñon mostly, not the tall, majestic ponderosas. Up in the mountains they had water and an occasional cool breeze, even in July. The McDowell Mountains could not compare to the White Mountains in Dylan's estimation. The air was so scalding here he felt as if he were fighting a wildfire. He rolled to a stop. The dust that had trailed him now swirled and settled on the shiny hood of his truck.

He rolled down the window of his white F-150 pickup and leaned out.

"Good morning," he called.

But instead of moving aside, she turned toward him and pressed both fists to her hips. The woman's clothing was tight, hugging her torso like a second skin. Was that a tennis outfit? She looked as if she had just spilled out of some exclusive country club. The woman wore her hair swept back, a clip holding the soft waves from her face so they tumbled to her shoulders. It was blue, a bright cobalt hue. Mostly, but there were other hues mixed in including deep purple, violet and turquoise.

It seemed the only protection she did use from the sun was the wide sunglasses that flashed gold at the edges. These she slipped halfway down her narrow nose as she regarded him at last with eyes the color of warm chocolate. She had lips tinted hot pink and her acrylic nails glowed a neon green that was usually reserved for construction attire. A sculpted brow arched in disapproval. Was there anything about her that was not artificial?

Dylan resisted the urge to glance at her breasts again.

"Mind moving your vehicle?" Dylan added a generous smile after his request. It was his experience that Anglo women were either wary of or curious about Apache men. This woman looked neither wary nor curious. She looked pissed.

Had her car broken down?

"You ruined my shot," she said, motioning at her tiny camera.

She was shooting in the direction he traveled, toward his destination, the house that broke the ridgeline and thus had caused so much controversy. Dylan had an appointment up there that could not be missed, one that marked a change in direction.

"The dust!" she said, and dropped a cloth over her camera.

"I'm sorry, ma'am." Dylan's years in the Marines had taught him many things, including how to address an angry Anglo woman. "But I have to get by. I have a meeting."

"I can't have you in the shot."

Was she refusing to move? Now Dylan's eyes narrowed.

"Are you unable to move that vehicle?" he asked.

"Unwilling."

She raised her pointed chin and Dylan felt an unwelcome tingle of desire. Oh, no. Heck, no—and no way, too. This woman was high maintenance and from a world he did not even recognize.

"You'll have to wait." Her mouth quirked as if she knew she was messing with him and was enjoying herself.

"But I have an appointment," he repeated.

"I don't give a fig."

"You can't just block a public road."

"Well, I guess I just did."

Dylan suppressed the urge to ram her Audi off into the rough. That's what his friend Ray Strong would do. Ray spent a lot of time cleaning up after his impulsiveness. Right now Dylan thought it might be worth it. He pictured the car sliding over the embankment and resisted the urge to smile.

"Do you know who I am?" she asked.

He lowered his chin and bit down to keep himself from telling her exactly what she was. Instead, he shook his head.

"I'm Meadow."

She gave only her first name, as if that was all that mattered. Not her family name or her tribe or clan. Just Meadow.

He shrugged one shoulder.

"Meadow Wrangler?"

He shook his head indicating his inability to place the name.

Her pretty little mouth dropped open.

"You don't know me?"

"Should I?" he asked.

"Only if you can read."

Charming, he thought.

In a minute he was getting out of his truck and she wouldn't like what happened next. He could move her and her camera without harming a blue hair on her obnoxious little head. Dylan gripped the door handle.

"My father is Theron Wrangler."

Dylan's hand fell from the handle and his eyes rounded.

She folded her arms. "Ah. You've heard of him."

He sure had, but likely not for the reason she thought. Theron Wrangler was the name that Amber Kitcheyan had overheard the day before the Lilac Copper Mine massacre. It was the name of the man that FBI field agent Luke Forrest believed was a member of the eco-extremist group known as BEAR, Bringing Earth Apocalyptic Restoration. But what was Theron Wrangler's profession?

"I'm not surprised. He won an Oscar at twenty-five. I'm working for him now. Documentary film on the impact of urban sprawl and on the construction of private residences that are environmental and aesthetic monstrosities." She motioned her head toward the mansion rising above the tree line on the ridge. "I've been here filming since construction. Timelapse. Sun up to sun down and today I finally have some clouds. Adds movement."

The wind was picking up, blowing grit and sand at them.

"I still need to get around you," said Dylan.

"And have your rooster tail in the shot? No way. Why are you going up there? I thought your people were protesting the building of that thing."

She was referring to the private residence of Gerald W. Rustkin, the man who had founded one of the social media sites that self-destructed all messages from either side of any conversation. The man who allowed others to hide had put himself in the center of controversy when he had donated generously to the city of Flagstaff and afterward quietly received his variances to break the ridgeline with his personal residence.

"My people?" asked Dylan.

"You're Native American, aren't you?"

"Yes, but we don't all think alike."

"But you're all environmentally conscious." she said, as if this was a given.

"That would be thinking alike."

"You don't want to prevent that thing from being built?" She pointed at the unfinished mansion sprawling over the top of the ridge like a serpent.

Dylan glanced at his watch. "I've got to go. You know you really should put on a hat."

She scoffed. "You think I'm worried about skin cancer? Nobody expects me to make thirty."

He wrinkled his brow. "Why not?" She looked healthy enough, but perhaps she was ill.

"Why?" She laughed. "You really don't know me?"

"Sorry."

"Don't be. It's refreshing. I'm the screwup. The family's black sheep. The party girl who forgot to wear her panties and broke the internet. I'm in the tabloids about every other week. Can't believe they didn't follow me out here. I thought you were one of them."

"I'm not."

"Yes, I can see that." She approached his truck. "Can't remember the last time I did this." She extended her hand. "I'm Meadow."

Dylan looked at her elegant hand. He considered

rolling up his window because this woman represented all the trouble he tried to avoid.

Instead, he took her hand gently between his fingers and thumb and gave it a little shake. But something happened. His smile became brittle and the gentle up-and-down motion of their arms ceased as he stared into bewitching amber-brown eyes. After an awkward pause he found his voice.

"Nice to meet you, Meadow. I'm Dylan Tehauno."

Her voice now sounded breathy. "A pleasure."

Her eyes glittered with mischief. Now he needed to get by her for other reasons, because this was the sort of woman you put behind you as quickly as possible.

She slipped her hand free and pressed her palm flat over her stomach. Were her insides jumping, like his?

"What's your business, Dylan?"

"I'm a hotshot."

She shook her head. "What's that, like a jet pilot?"

"I fight wildfires. Forest fires. We fly all over the West—Idaho, Oregon, Colorado. Even east once to Tennessee. Man, is it green there."

"Really? So you jump out of airplanes with an ax. That kind of thing?"

"No, those are smoke jumpers. We walk in. Sometimes twenty miles from deployment. Then we get to work." In fact, he had most of his gear in the box fixed to the bed of his truck.

"That's crazy."

He thought standing in the sun with a GoPro was crazy, but he just smiled. "Gotta go."

"All right, Sir Dylan. You may pass. How long will you be up there?"

"Hour maybe."

"Time enough for me to get my shot then." She reversed course and moved her tripod behind her sports car.

Dylan rolled past. He couldn't stop from glancing at her in the rearview mirror. He kept looking back until she was out of sight. Soon he started the ascent to the house, winding through the thick pines and dry grasses.

His shaman and the leader of his medicine society, Kenshaw Little Falcon, had recommended Dylan for this job. This was his first commission in Flagstaff. He'd recently earned his credentials as a fire-safety inspector in Arizona. As a fire consultant, it was usually his role to give recommendations to protect the home from wildfire, identify places where wildfire might trap or kill people and provide fuel-reduction plans. Something as simple as trimming the branches of trees from the ground to at least ten feet or not placing mulch next to the house could be the difference between losing a home and saving it. But this consultation was different because so many did not want this house completed. Cheney Williams, the attorney who had filed the injunction, waited for him on the ridge. Dylan felt important because he knew that his report might prevent the multimillionaire Rustkin from securing insurance. At the very least it would buy time. That would be a feather in Dylan's cap. He lowered his arm out his window and patted the magnetic sign affixed to the door panel—Tehauno Consulting.

Dylan smiled and then glanced back to the road where he could no longer see Meadow Wrangler. He should be looking ahead. By the time he finished with the attorney, would Meadow be gone?

The flash of light was so bright that for an instant everything went white. Dylan hit the brakes. The boom arrived a moment later, shaking the truck and vibrating through his hands where they gripped the wheel. Artillery.

His brain snapped to Iraq. He had served two tours and he knew the sound of an explosion. He glanced up, looking for the jets that could make such an air strike and saw the debris fly across the ridgeline. A fireball erupted skyward and rained burning embers down from above. Rocks pelted the road before him.

Meadow.

Dylan made a fast three-point turn and was hurtling down the mountain as embers landed all about him, erupting into flames. It was July, over a hundred degrees today, and the ground was as dry and thirsty as it had been all year. Perfect conditions for a wildfire. But this was not one wildfire—it was hundreds. Burning debris landed and ignited as if fueled by a propellant. The flames traveled as fast as he did. Faster, because the wind raced down the mountain, pushing the growing wall of flames that licked at the trunks of the piñon pines. Once it hit the crowns of the trees it would take off. There was nothing to stop it. His only chance was to get ahead of it and stay there.

MEADOW GAPED AS the top of the ridge exploded like an erupting volcano. With her camera still running, she stood in the road, paralyzed by what she witnessed. The house that had broken the ridgeline collapsed, falling in fiery wreckage into the gap below. The steel skeleton vanished amid tails of smoke that flew into the sky like launching rockets.

Dylan.

He was up there. Her impulse was to flee, but the urge to reach him tugged against her survival instinct.

The rockets of fire flew over her head, and she turned to watch them land, each a meteor impacting the earth. The vibrations from the explosion reached her, tipping her camera and making her sidestep to keep from falling beside it. She lifted the running GoPro and held it, collapsing the tripod as she panned, capturing the flaming rock touching down and igniting infernos to her right and left, knowing the HDMI video interface and antenna in her car compressed the video data before sending it to the live feed.

The desert bloomed orange as it burned. She turned back to the ridge, seeing the smoke billowing up to the sun. Beneath the yellow smoke came a wall of fire and the cracking, popping sound of burning. A hot wind rushed at her, burning her skin. She felt as if she stood in an oven. She had to get out of here. Meadow turned in a circle and saw flames on all sides. The smoke was so thick she began to choke. Should she try to drive through the flames?

How had the falling rock and fire missed her? She stood in the road as she realized everyone had been right. She wasn't going to see thirty.

Chapter Two

Had she gotten out? Dylan wondered as he barely managed to navigate his truck along the thin ribbon of gravel to the bottom of the ridge and onto the straight stretch that led to Meadow.

He prayed that she had, but the fear in his heart and the flames already crowning in the pines warned him she was in danger. He listened to his instincts, slowed his speed, fighting against the urge to accelerate. Moving faster than he could see could cause him to crash the truck or to hit Meadow. He was close to her position now. He knew it. Where was she?

He saw her Audi parked exactly where it had been—only now the wall of fire to his left glimmered off the mirror surface of the black paint reflecting the approaching flames. Soon the paint would melt, along with every bit of plastic. The inferno was close to jumping the road. Dylan hit the brakes, sending gravel spraying from his rear tires.

"Meadow!" he shouted as he threw open the door. "Meadow!"

The blaze was loud now, sounding like a locomotive. His eyes burned as he swept the ground for any sight of her. Then he saw a flash of white. She was running. Strong legs pumping as she darted from behind her car and then in front of his truck. In one hand she held her camera by the folded, compressed tripod. She reached the passenger side, and his arms went around her instinctively as he pulled her into the truck and set them in motion again.

Not here, he thought. There was too much fuel. Too much energy for the flames to consume in the surrounding pines.

"There's no way out," she shouted.

He knew that. He knew they were trapped. It was not a question of if but when the fire would catch them.

Not here. Not yet.

He glanced behind them. The fire glowed red in the rearview. So close now. Ahead there was only smoke and the orange flames that raced along on either side of the road. Finally he saw it. The black earth he had been searching for. The fire had already burned the easy fuel there. He glanced back. How long did he have? A few minutes. He needed more earth, more black earth between him and what chased them. He needed a place to survive the burn-over.

He went as far as he could, hoping, praying it was far enough. Knowing if he went any farther he would not have the moments he needed to prepare.

Dylan hit the brakes.

"What are you doing?" yelled Meadow. "Go! Go!"

He reached across the gap between them and dragged her out of the truck by her wrist. She didn't fight him, just locked her jaw and allowed him to pull her behind him. He grabbed his rake and thrust it at her. She clutched it in her free hand, the other still gripping her camera. Then he seized his pack and Pulaski ax from the utility storage box in his truck bed. No time to talk. No room for the bottles of water he always carried. He glanced about as he judged the wind and the flames, wishing the crowns of the trees had already burned. Then he rushed them off the embankment to the black earth. The road would help break the flames, but the truck… Were they far enough to be clear of the gas tanks? He tugged her along, running into the smoking black soil that crunched beneath his construction boots. Choosing his spot because he was out of time, he went to work with the ax breaking the soil, tearing away the burned vegetation by the roots, digging a trench. The ground was so hot. He'd never thought he'd have to deploy his fire shelter. After all the training films and practice and all the fires he had fought, Dylan really had believed that he could control the situation, stay ahead of the fire line and always have a viable escape plan. Yet, here he was.

"What are you doing?" she yelled.

The roar was louder and the hot wind rushed past them.

"Rake that away!" he yelled.

He broke more soil, digging deeper and glancing at the approaching wall of flame.

She pushed the tripod down the front of her shirt before using the fire rake to pull away the roots and brush he cleared with the ax.

"A grave?" she asked.

He paused to stare at her. She looked back with a calm that terrified him because he saw that she was ready to die.

"Fire shelter," he called.

Her brows lifted and he could not tell if she was relieved or disappointed.

No time now.

"That comes off." He tugged at her shirt.

"What?"

"Polyester. It melts." He dragged the shirt over her head. She dropped the rake. The camera tumbled free, and she stooped to her knees to snatch it up again and yelped at the contact of her bare knee with the smoking ground. He went for his pack, grabbing the flame-retardant shirt he wore to fight fires and tugged it on. It would be *his* back between the shelter and the flames.

"This, too?" She lifted the edge of the flimsy scrap of fabric that was her skirt.

He nodded and dropped the camel pack in the ditch, then took his gloves and radio, but nothing else. He'd never heard of two people deploying in a shelter that was designed for one.

He estimated the wind was reaching fifty miles an hour now. If he lost the shelter to the wind they were both dead. He dropped to his knees, already tugging the fire shelter from the nylon sheath.

"That looks like a Jiffy Pop bag," she said.

"Come!" he roared.

She dropped before him and he enveloped her, forcing her down to the earth and into the shallow ditch he had made. The roar grew louder, like a jet engine that went on and on.

He got the shelter over them and used the hand straps to tug the edges about them. His feet slid inside the elastic and he braced, holding himself up on his elbows.

"It's hot," she called, wriggling. "The ground—it's too hot. I'm burning."

"Stay still." It was hotter outside, he knew. Five hundred degrees and rising, he thought, his training providing him the information.

"This isn't going to stop it. It's thin as one of those emergency blankets."

Except this was two-ply. A silicon layer and the reflective outer foil.

"We'll cook alive!" she yelled.

It was possible. Not all deployed wildfire fighters survived. But mostly they died from the heated gases that scorched their lungs until they could not breathe.

"Stick your face in the dirt and take shallow breaths," he shouted in her ear to be heard above the roar. The explosion that shook them told him that his truck tires had blown. The gas tank would be next. Flying debris could rip the shelter. If that happened, they would die here.

The fire shield now seemed a living thing that he had to wrestle to hold down about them. The heat intensified until he felt as if the skin on his back burned. Every time the shelter touched him, it seared. He kept his elbows pinned and punched at the shelter, creating an air space. Each breath scalded his lungs. He took shallow sips of air and held them as long as possible, hoping the next breath would not be his last.

MEADOW FELT THE weight of him pressing down upon her. He was so big and the ground so hot. She couldn't breathe.

"We have to get out," she yelled, not knowing if he heard her. The air in her next breath was so hot she choked. He pushed her head down to the ground.

"Dig!" he ordered.

She held the neck of the tripod and used the collapsed legs to dig, making a hole, and then she released her GoPro to cup her hands over her face to inhale. How could he even breathe? The air above her head was even hotter. He needed to get his face down by hers.

She dug faster, using her hands now, her acrylic nails raking soft sand as she burrowed like a ground squirrel. "You, too!"

She gasped at the intake of hot air into her throat.

He wriggled forward, his cheek now beside hers, his nose and lips pressing into her cupped hands. She could feel his shallow breath. Their skin was hot and damp where their cheeks met.

From somewhere outside the balloon shelter came an explosion. She flinched.

Chapter Three

"Gas tank," he shouted, clarifying what had just blown up.

The roaring went on and the shield fluttered and bucked, reminding her of the slack sail on a sailboat.

Ready about, her father would call, and the boom would swing over her head. As the smallest and quickest, she was allowed to scramble up to the foredeck to tie off the lines and drop the buoy between the ship and the dock.

Something stung her chest. She clawed at her bra.

"Burning," she cried.

Dylan lifted, released the back fastening as she tugged it clear.

"Metal heats up," he shouted in her ear. "Buttons, rivets."

Underwire, she thought. The thing was so hot, like a brand against her flesh. She wondered if she had burned her skin. If she could just lift the edge of the cover and get some air. But he held it down with his forearms and legs. She reached for the shelter and he grabbed her wrist, forcing it to the hot, black earth.

"I need to breathe!" she shouted.

He said nothing. Just held her down along with the tinfoil roaster bag that was cooking them alive. It was an oven. Hotter than an oven. She pressed her face back in the dirt and tried to breathe through the fingers of her free hand. The rings were heating. She tugged at her captured hand. He resisted.

"My rings. Burning!"

He released her and she jerked off her silver, gold and platinum rings and pushed them away.

Beams of red light shone down in narrow shafts through the cover. She glanced up. There were holes in the shelter. She pointed and felt him nod.

"It will be all right," he said. "It will still work."

Had the roaring decreased? She wasn't sure.

"How you doing?" he asked.

She could hear him now. He wasn't shouting.

"I don't want to die," she whispered. The words came as a surprise to her. Yesterday there was nothing she'd wanted to do. Nowhere she'd wanted to go. And now she just wanted to see the sky again. Dive into cold water. Inhale the scent of peonies.

"We're both going to live." He brushed his cheek against hers. "I'll keep you safe, Meadow. It won't get you."

She closed her eyes and struggled to control the ball of pain that tried to escape her throat as a sob. She failed. Here she had thought there was only a thin veil of foil between her and the fire. But it wasn't so. Dylan stood between her and the flames. He protected her with his body and his promise, and she loved him for it.

"How long do we have to stay in here?"

He shifted, letting his hip slide to the ground, taking some of his weight from her. "A while. Have to be sure it's past us."

"How will you know?"

"The sound. The roar is fading. The heat and the color. It's orange now. See?"

She lifted her head to the pinholes and saw the light that had been pink and then red like the flashing light of a fire engine were now the orange of glowing coals. The sky shouldn't be that color. Never, ever. She let her head fall back to the breathing hole.

He stuck something against her face.

"Drink," he ordered.

It was a tube. She put it in her mouth and swallowed. Water—hot, stale and welcome. She drank until he took the hose from her. How much water had she lost in this tinfoil tent?

She marveled at him. In only minutes he had gathered from the truck exactly what they needed to survive.

"How do you know all this? How do you have one of these things?" *Hotshot*, she remembered. Walking twenty miles to deploy, he'd said. She needed to get one of these Jiffy Pop thingies. "You fight wildfires," she said, more to herself than to him.

"Yes."

"Dylan?"

"Hmm?"

She wished she could look at him, see his handsome face, those dark eyes and the clean line of his jaw, but he was so close that his nose was pressed to her ear and he lay half across her.

"Can you…talk to me? You know? Take my mind off…"

"What about?"

"Tell me about yourself."

"Well, I told you my name. I'm from the Turquoise Canyon Apache tribe. We are Tonto Apache. I live up there on the reservation between Antelope Lake and Darabee in the mountains."

His voice was like a song with a lyrical quality that calmed her. She felt the panic easing away as he continued.

"If I met you there I would say to you, 'Hello, I am Bear, born of Butterfly, and my father's name is Jonathan Tehauno. My mother's name is Dorothy Florez. They named me Dylan.' It's more important there to know your parents and clans. Your name comes after all that or sometimes not at all. So when I say, 'Bear, born of Butterfly,' you know my father's clan is Bear and my mother's clan is Butterfly."

"I live in Phoenix. I am Wrangler, born of Theron and Lupe. My mother's name was Cortez."

He chuckled and she felt herself smile.

"Tell me more." She felt herself relaxing, her weary muscles twitching from the tension that now eased away into the hot earth.

"I live in the community of Koun'nde in tribal housing. My friends make fun of me because my home has so many books."

She chuckled because she had stopped reading the minute she realized no one could make her do anything.

"I own a truck, nearly, and have five horses in the community herd. Well, I did own a truck." He sighed and then coughed. After a moment he kept talking, his breath cool against her face. "I like to ride. I've won some endurance races on horses and on foot. After high school, I joined the US Marines. I was honorably discharged after two tours. Decided not to reenlist. I missed home. It's cool up on the mountain. Not like down here in Flagstaff or over in the Sandbox. That's what we called Iraq."

His voice hummed in her ear, a deep, resonant song. She closed her watering eyes.

"Let's see. I'm a member of a medicine society, the Turquoise Guardians. We dance at festivals and perform ceremonies. I sing in a drum circle."

She didn't know what any of that meant, but she wanted him to keep talking.

"The people say I have a good voice."

Meadow agreed with that, though she had not heard him sing. She wanted to ask him, but it was so hard for her just to breathe, she didn't have the heart.

"I've been trying to get some of my friends to join me in August to go up to Rapid City for the Indian Relay Races. We'd need four good horses and a four-man team. One rider and each horse runs one mile with the same rider."

She tried to picture that, one man leaping from one horse to another.

"I keep telling Jack that he was born to be a catcher and Ray and Carter could hold the mounts. I'd like to ride, but if they're faster I'd let them go, instead. Only now Carter's in witness protection. So we need a fourth. I suggested Carter's brother Kurt. He's smaller but strong. Jack said he'd think about it. Jack Bear Den is a detective on our tribal police. His brother Carter and my friend Ray Strong are hotshots. Turquoise Canyon Hotshots. That's us. Kurt Bear Den is a paramedic with the air ambulance. I've been a hotshot since I came home but it's only six months, the fire season. So I need more work. I was supposed to meet Cheney Williams."

Her eyes popped open. "I know him."

"You do?"

"He works with my dad. He's a financial guy for the documentaries. Contracts, I think. Something. I'm not really sure. He's around a lot." Meadow felt a rumble in Dylan's chest, like a growl.

"I was told that he's an attorney in environmental law. Working to stop that house."

"You haven't met him?"

"No. My shaman recommended me."

She lifted her chin. It was easier to breathe. "Was he up there?"

The rough stubble on his chin brushed her temple. "Probably. He was meeting me there."

"Do you think he got out?"

Silence was her answer.

"Who would do this?"

His body tensed. "I'm planning to find that out."

"The whole ridge exploded. The rocks were flying everywhere. I can't believe they didn't hit me." She told him everything. About how she was filming and the red fireball and the house collapsing and the trees ablaze.

"You filmed the whole thing?"

"Yes."

"Why were you here today?"

"I've been here several times during the construction. My father sent me. He has a shooting schedule." She didn't say that her dad hadn't used any of the footage she'd shot. That she was beginning to think her assignment was a snipe hunt, designed to be rid of her, keep her busy and out of the clubs. That last headline had embarrassed them. Too much attention, her mother had said.

Too much was better than none at all, she thought, and she lowered her head.

"Your father sent you here. Today."

She didn't like the way he said that.

"Well, he couldn't have known this would happen."

His silence was her only answer. Meadow frowned. She didn't like that silence. There was something sinister and judgmental about it.

"My father is a saint. He's spent his whole life raising awareness of really important issues with his films."

Still no reply.

"What are you implying?" she asked.

"Heck of a coincidence."

"I could say the same for you."

"Yes. That occurred to me," he said.

The hairs on her neck lifted. She felt the need to fill the silence.

"Lucky you were here," she said.

"Yeah." There was a long pause. "Lucky."

"You saved my life."

"Not yet, I haven't." He moved again, trying his radio and getting nothing but static. He slipped the antenna out from under the fire shield and tried again. This time he got through to someone and she heard him give their position and ask for assistance. He also asked them to contact Detective Jack Bear Den on Turquoise Canyon Reservation.

He retracted the radio antenna inside the shield and she saw the black plastic tip had melted.

"I guess my car and Wi-Fi antenna is toast."

"You have internet out here?"

"I did. I was streaming my footage."

"You captured the explosion and streamed it... where?"

"My social media. Vine, Snapchat, Instagram. I also have YouTube, Facebook and Google+ and send footage to my remote server."

He went very still. "So anyone could see what you shot."

"Yes. That's the point."

"So you don't need to make it out of here alive for someone to see what you saw."

The hairs on her neck now began to tingle.

"What are you saying?"

"I think you and I were sent here to die."

Chapter Four

Dylan tried to put the pieces together. He didn't know if he was injured. During the worst of the burn-over he'd felt as if the skin on his back had burned. He knew from his training that it was not uncommon for a deployed hotshot to suffer burns. But the shelters worked. And theirs *had* worked. They were alive and the worst had passed. The worst of the firestorm. But now he wondered if by sending a distress call he had alerted whoever had sent them that they had survived. Radio channels were easy to monitor. If his hunch was right, they needed to get out of here before help arrived because the worst of the firestorm might still be out there.

The vehicles would be useless. He'd heard the tires blow and both gas tanks explode. His poor truck. He didn't even own it yet. Meadow would likely have a new Audi by morning.

If they lived that long.

Help was coming, but so too were the ones who had set that explosive. Dylan was sure.

"Tell me what's happening," she demanded.

Was she one of them? A WOLF or a BEAR?

WOLF, Wilderness of Land Forever, was the less rad-
icalized arm of the eco-extremists, who destroyed
property but only if it did not jeopardize human life.
BEAR made no such allowances. The FBI thought
her father was a member of BEAR, perhaps the head
of the eco-extremist group. Jack had told him that.
But they hadn't proved it—not yet.

Had she been sent here as a sacrificial lamb, to die
for the cause as a martyr?

He remembered that look when she'd asked him if
he was digging their grave. She'd been ready.

"Did you come here to die?"

"What?" she said. She made a scoffing sound and
then gave a halfhearted laugh.

Dylan felt his upper arm tingle. Not because of the
heat outside the shelter but because of the tattoo he had
gotten after joining Tribal Thunder, the warrior sect
of his medicine society. His shaman had suggested
each new member have a spirit animal to help guide
them. It was Ray Strong's idea to have them branded
on their skin. Dylan's spirit animal was bobcat, and
his tattoo was the track of the bobcat on a medicine
shield, beneath which hung five eagle feathers. He
loved having a cat as his guide but did not appreciate
the reason. His shaman said Dylan was too overt and
needed to be aware that not all things operated on the
surface. Bobcat would help him see what was hidden
and give him a quality he lacked—stealth.

Dylan had a reputation for being where he was supposed to be and doing what was expected, more than
was expected. He wasn't reckless like Ray Strong or
suspicious like Jack Bear Den or a natural leader like

Jack's twin brother, Carter. He was predictable and he followed the rules. He was the conscience of the group. Was that so bad?

This woman beneath him was not what she seemed. A shadow figure. Appearing one thing while being another or existing on two planes at the same time. A woman with two faces. He felt it and Bobcat warned him to be cautious.

"Have you heard of an organization called WOLF, or one called BEAR?" he asked, and then kicked himself for the overt question. But how would he know the answer if he could not ask?

BEAR was much worse. Bringing Earth Apocalyptic Restoration. That group was eco-terrorists. They'd orchestrated the mass shooting at the Lilac Copper Mine to cover the long-term theft of mining supplies and then paid a member of his tribe to kill the gunman of the mass murder, breaking the link between the gunman and those who sent him.

"WOLF? Yes. They burned that Jeep outfit in Sedona. Right? Some kind of activist opposed to overdevelopment of the land. Can hardly blame them. Damn red Hummers rolling all over the fragile ecosystem." Her mouth dropped open. She must have inhaled some of the sand on her face because she coughed and spit. Then she turned, trying to glance back at him. They were so close he could feel every muscle in her back tense. So close he could press his lips to her temple.

"You think they did this?" she asked.

He did not reply, but he could almost hear her mind working.

"But the fire. They must have known that would

cause a fire. And they don't destroy the land. They protect it. And the explosion. That was like something from a movie."

"Or a mine," Dylan said.

"Lilac."

There had been no mention of the loss of mining supplies from the Lilac mine in the media. Yet she had made the connection with the speed of a lightning strike. Mines had explosives, blasting cord and everything you needed to do exactly what they had just both witnessed.

He swallowed as he accepted the confirmation. Why did he think she could not be one of them? Because she was pretty or pampered or seemingly suffering from a terminal case of affluenza? Bobcat would see through all that. Bobcat would proceed slowly without moving a single blade of grass.

Her father, Theron Wrangler, was the one person the FBI had successfully linked to BEAR because Amber Kitcheyan, an employee at Lilac and the only survivor, had heard that name spoken the day before the shooting. Dylan's friend Carter Bear Den had rescued her and the FBI now had both of them in protective custody.

This woman was Theron's daughter and she'd captured the explosion on film, then streamed it live. He thought of the suicide bombers in the Middle East. Had she planted those explosives?

"We have to get out of here," Dylan said.

"I'm all for that."

He glanced up at the holes in his fire shelter—the

required equipment he had purchased a year ago and never expected to need. His crew was too careful, too experienced and too smart to be trapped by the living, breathing monster of a wildfire.

He dragged the camel pack from beneath his knees and drank, then offered Meadow a drink. Some deployed men suffered from dehydration, and, unable to leave the shelter as their bodies had lost too much vital fluids, they died. He was lucky to have had the seconds he needed to grab the water pouch.

Dylan thought about his truck and the sturdy utility box made of a polymer and likely now a melted lump of plastic. All his equipment and the water— gone.

He resisted the urge to lift the shelter as he estimated the temperature inside had reached over two hundred degrees and was now falling. Every rock and stone beneath them radiated heat like the bricks in a pizza oven.

"Couldn't it have been a gas explosion?" she asked.

"No gas lines."

"Welding tanks, for construction?"

"Maybe." Let her think that. He'd seen gas tanks explode on training videos. They were impressive but could not melt steel and bring down a 4500-square-foot home.

Dylan debated what to do. If he stayed, it gave whoever picked up his radio transmission time to get to them.

What would his friend Ray Strong do? Ray was the crazy one, or he had been until he met Morgan Hooke and became responsible for a woman and her child. Ray had changed. Perhaps his spirit animal, eagle, had really helped him see clearly and act, not on impulse, but with clarity and purpose.

Jack Bear Den would tell Dylan to be careful. To act on the assumption that the worst was coming and to be ready.

Jack's twin, Carter Bear Den, would tell Dylan to be ready to fight what came. Carter's tattoo was a bear track. Bears were strong. Carter had needed that strength to leave his tribe and go with the woman he loved. What would Carter do? He'd been their captain for the Turquoise Canyon Hotshots, a job Dylan assumed when Carter left them in February. They would be deploying without him today. He was sure. Who would be leading them now?

Dylan had joined the Turquoise Canyon Hotshots after his discharge. He had four full seasons fighting wildfire and two months and three fires as captain. But none like this. Back then fighting wildfire had been exciting. He had felt immortal. But his tours of duty in Iraq had shown him that none of them were and, lately, he had felt the weight of being the leader of his team. His decisions meant the life or death of members of his crew and he found himself questioning his ability to lead.

He held the shelter, feeling the time race by with the wind. If he was right and they stayed here too long, someone would come to finish what the fire had started. If they left too early, the heat would burn their lungs, saving the team from BEAR the trouble of killing them.

"How much longer?" asked Meadow.

The sand and grit stuck to her damp skin. She'd never been so thirsty and she was beginning to feel dizzy.

"A few minutes more." He glanced at her. "Why don't you tell me about yourself? Pass the time." And get to know the enemy beside him. Bobcat would be pleased.

"Well, okay. I'm Meadow. My mom's nickname for me is Dodo, if that's any hint. You know, like the bird? I'm the last of six children. The oops baby. My next oldest sister, Katrina, is seven years my senior. My oldest brother, Phillip, is the CEO of PAN. My three sisters, Connie, short for Consuelo, Rosalie, Katrina, and my other brother, Miguel, are all professionals with promising careers." She had started to use air quotes but then dropped her hands back to the hot earth and the tripod.

Being so much younger sometimes made her feel like she was an only child with six parents.

"I'm closest to Katrina. She looked out for me when she could, or she used to before…you know, when I was a kid."

And when Meadow was home, which wasn't often.

"Your name isn't Spanish," said Dylan.

"What? No, it isn't."

"The others are, and your mother, Lupe."

She'd never really thought of that before.

"Anyway. Phillip is a CEO. Miguel is a doctor. So is Connie, Consuelo. Rosalie is an attorney and Kat has a business degree from Berkeley, undergrad and a law degree from…" She tapped her chin. "I forget where… Anyway, just passed the bar. They all went to private school here. Me, too, for a while. I got kicked out. I also got kicked out of schools in Westchester, Greenwich, Boston and Vermont."

"That's a lot of schools."

"What can I say? I'm good at what I do."

"So you cause trouble. Make a big fuss so everyone notices you."

"That's it." Only they didn't. Not often.

But getting sent home was the one sure way to get her father's attention.

"Oh, and colleges, too. I went to NYU for film. My dad made a contribution because my grades, well… I tried to be a chip off the old block. But my brothers have that gig all tied up. So I went to Berkeley for economics and then UCLA for marine biology."

"How'd you do?"

"I got mostly A's on the tests I took. Problem was I didn't take enough of them. I had trouble getting to class."

"Failed out?"

"Every time."

"But all A's. You're smart."

"If I was smart, would I be lying under an Apache hotshot in the middle of a wildfire?"

"Good point."

"Maybe I'll go back to school. They have some in Hawaii. I could learn to surf."

"How old are you?"

"Twenty-six, but I'll be twenty-seven next month. Just in time to join the 27 Club."

"What's that?"

She turned to stare at him in disbelief. "You got to get off your mountain. Get your brain out of the smoke."

"Maybe. So…the 27 Club?"

"It's all the musicians who died at twenty-seven. Morrison, Hendrix, Joplin, Cobain, Winehouse. Only they were famous for creating something and I'm only famous for being the screw-up daughter of a rich man. Creating scandals. I haven't done anything else."

"Not too late," he said.

"Yeah. I'd like to see twenty-eight, even thirty."

He tugged her closer to him, adjusting his body to hold the shelter.

"Can I help hold it down?" she asked, and then realized this was the very first time she'd offered to do anything. She'd drunk his water, complained about the lifesaving shelter and whined about how hard it was to breathe. She sagged. Maybe he should have rolled her out from under the shelter like a log. She knew she would have been tempted if their situation had been reversed.

"You'd need gloves. The edges get hot."

Yet the thing had been flapping against him for what seemed like hours. He'd never uttered a word of complaint.

"How old are you?" she asked.

"Twenty-eight."

He seemed older, acted older, she realized.

"I'm going to lift the shield," he said. "Hold your breath."

Meadow drew as deep a breath as she could in the scalding hot air as Dylan lifted the edge of the shelter.

Chapter Five

A blast of hot winds rushed in below the fire shelter. The burning air made Meadow's eyes tear.

"Everything is black," she said, releasing her breath and then gasping at the heat of the air now rushing into her lungs. She hurried to be rid of it. The next breath seemed just as hot.

"Good. Did you see any fire?"

"No." She pressed her hands over her stinging eyes and rubbed. "Hot."

"Don't rub them. Just keep your eyes closed."

After a few minutes he asked her to hold the edge of the shelter. She tried but the metal was too hot. He piled some sand on the inner edge and she was able to press down the lip with her palm.

He used his free hand to retrieve his radio. She gaped at the melted top to the antenna. What did her car look like? It was miles to anything. A new fear tripped her heart rate. They couldn't walk out. It was too far.

"Help is coming. Right?" she asked.

"Someone will be here as soon as it's safe." He

lifted the edge again. The air was hot, but not as hot. "Stay here."

"What! No!"

"Meadow, I'm wearing boots, a fire-resistant shirt, cotton jeans. You're naked."

That was true.

"Stay here until I tell you."

She nodded. "Be careful."

He slid off one glove. "Put that on. Use it to hold the shelter down. Use your feet to hold the bottom edge."

With that, he lifted the right side and rolled away. The edge flapped as she tried and failed to catch it. She felt as if her skin blistered. From outside the shelter the edge dropped and she was able to get her gloved hand down on the perimeter.

"Feet!" he yelled.

She spread her legs until her sandaled feet were in place. Meadow tried and failed to ignore the pain of her burning toes.

"Stay there," he called from outside the shield.

She heard the crunch of his feet on the scorched earth. Meadow's legs and arms began to tremble from the effort of keeping the shelter steady against the constant wind. How had he held the shield down all that time? It seemed impossible. Again she realized that Dylan Tehauno had saved her life. She knew he had come back just for her, and, because of that act, everything in her life that was good was a gift from him.

Meadow's eyes burned and she was surprised she had enough water left in her body to cry. But the tears came, sliding over the bridge of her nose and dropping into the dry sand. Even the tears were thanks to

Dylan. The sobs came next. Meadow was so grateful and so undeserving.

How did a person like her repay a man like him? Money? Sex? A new truck? He said he was looking for a job. She could help him with that. Her father employed lots of people. Her brother Phillip, too. If she asked, her dad would give Dylan a job. Especially when he found out what he had done. She needed to call her father. But her phone was in her car. Or it had been.

The crunch of his boots signaled his return.

"Meadow. I'm taking off the shield."

The foil wrapper lifted away and the hot air rushed past her. She pressed her hands over her mouth to cool the next breath as she rolled to her side looking up at him.

He stood shirtless, his skin smudged with ash and glistening with sweat. Dylan dropped his shirt over her naked body.

"Put that on."

She drew to her knees, tugging the garment over her shoulders and holding it closed before her. The sand stuck to her skin and poured under her sandals. He offered his hand and, looking around, she rose beside him. The fire now raced far back along the road she had traveled, a line of orange glowing beneath the billowing gray smoke.

They were surrounded by a forest of tree trunks charred black and smoking. How many animals had died in that fire? She shivered at the thought. How many houses in the valley below them were now at risk? She'd driven through a new development that butted against the national forest. She remembered her father complaining about the expensive homes positioned with views of the sunset over the ridge. He'd called them hypocrites because they had objected to the mansion that broke the ridgeline for obstructing *their* views.

They were likely evacuating now.

Meadow glanced at the trench he had made. There lay the only patch of earth devoid of flammable vegetation. The only place the earth was not black. Her pink lace bra lay in the sand and a diamond on one of her rings twinkled. Then she spotted her GoPro. She stooped to recover it and paused. The camera was intact, but the tripod had not been wholly under the shelter and it had melted to a lump of black plastic. She stared at the evidence of how much hotter it had been outside the shelter than inside. Dylan crouched beside her and offered a wet bandanna, and she washed her face, horrified at the black soot that came away on the red cotton. He rinsed the cloth and used it to wipe off her throat. The simple act of kindness undid her.

She turned to him and fell into his arms, sobbing. He stroked her tangled hair. He whispered to her in a language she could not understand as she clung to him and wept. His hand stroked her back, rubbing up and down over the shirt he had given her. Everything she had and everything she was she owed to him. She lifted her chin to look up at him.

Why hadn't she seen the kindness in his dark eyes or the strength reflected in his blade of a nose and the strong line of his jaw rough with dark stubble and sand? All she'd seen was a nuisance ruining her shot.

His black brows lifted and the corner of his mouth twitched upward. That mouth was so tempting and she was so lost.

Meadow threaded one hand in his thick, short hair and tugged, angling her chin, and rose onto her toes, pressing her mouth to his.

DYLAN STARTLED AT the unexpected contact and the unprecedented wave of desire that swept over him. Reflexively, his arms contracted, drawing her tight to his chest. Only after the contact of her bare skin to his did he remember she had not yet buttoned his shirt and he had removed his T-shirt to check his back for burns. Her bare breasts molded to the hard planes of his chest, setting off a firestorm inside his body. Her tongue flicked out and he opened his mouth, allowing her to deepen the kiss that soon consumed them both. When her fingers scored his bare back, Dylan's need overwhelmed him, but the fluttering in his belly and the stirring below that did not quite overtake the whisper of danger.

Bobcat growled a warning.

The overt. Her seeming desire.

The hidden. Her real purpose. Was this a distraction to give her people time to reach them? A way to make him forget his unease and take what she offered?

She had told him she was a party girl. Now he saw her provocative nature. Sex to this woman meant no more than choosing what dessert to eat. Dylan pushed her away, not because of the danger or the hidden agenda but because he did not wish to be the flavor of the month. For him, the intimacy shared by man and woman was sacred.

"We need to go," he said.

She looked up at him with wide eyes, and a enticing pink mouth opened just enough to tempt him to kiss her again. But he wouldn't, precisely because he did want to so much. She seemed bewildered. Oh, this one was good. Very, very good. If he did not know better, he would believe the innocence and astonishment he saw in her face.

"Come on. Now."

He drew her away from him and then let her go. He allowed himself one long look at the swath of bare skin revealed between the edges of his shirt. His gaze stopped on the scrap of pink lace that covered her seemingly hairless sex. Then he met her gaze and saw the power in her eyes. She was used to men looking at her like this, completely comfortable now, as if she had regained her footing and stood on familiar ground. She stared at him with a kind of triumph melded with seduction.

He pointed at his shirt. "Button that."

Meadow gave a mock salute that revealed the bottom curve of a bare breast. Dylan met her gaze.

"Why did you do that?" he asked, brushing the sand from his chest and tugging on his T-shirt.

"I just wanted to thank you."

He shoved his bandanna in the back pocket of his jeans. "You don't thank a man by having sex with him, Meadow."

"Sometimes I do."

"I'm not like you, then. I'm not casual about such things."

"A real Boy Scout," she said, pink lips curling.

"You should have more pride and respect for yourself."

He saw his condemnation strike her. Her bottom lip quivered. Was this an act or real emotion? He rubbed his right shoulder, wishing Bobcat could tell him because his instinct was to take her in his arms again. Ridiculous. She was a wealthy, spoiled, lost womanchild and he was not interested.

Dylan dug in the sand, recovering her rings. "How many did you have?"

"Four." She accepted the offering in cupped palms and slipped the trinkets onto her long fingers.

Meadow looked from her hand to the ground.

"Is that your ax?" She pointed at the metal head that was all that remained of the Pulaski ax after the wood had burned away.

He lifted the ax head and then dropped it back to the sand.

"Fought a lot of fires with that. Like losing an old friend."

Meadow glanced to the road to the two burned hulls that had been his truck and her car. They were scorched gray and looked old, ancient, as if abandoned years and years ago.

She gasped, pressing one hand to her mouth as she pointed with the other.

"My car!"

"Totaled. But I suspect you have it fully insured."

She took a step closer. "The glass melted. The seats. Upholstery. Everything." Meadow gaped at him. "All the paint just… It looks like… Why is it on its side?"

"Gas tank must have been full."

"I topped it up on Canyon Road before coming out here." She lifted her digital recorder. All the acrylic nails had popped off her fingers in the heat, leaving small, ragged, natural nails glowing pink on her blackened, dirty fingers. She fiddled with the buttons and the screen illuminated. "It still works!"

She beamed at him.

"We have to go," he said.

"But you called for help. They might be here soon."

If they could get through the fire wall and if the ones who came were here to help them, he would stay. But there was too much risk. Rescue might be hours, even days, away, and the ones who had started this fire might reach them first.

"You can stay. I'm walking out." He turned and headed in the direction of the ridgeline, some two miles away.

"What? Wait up." She trotted along with him over the smoking ground. "Wow. It's really hot. I can feel it right through the soles of my sandals."

He stopped and debated. If he was wrong and she was not involved, they might kill her. If he was right and he brought her along, then she could report back to them everything he said and did.

"What?" she asked, those bright golden-brown eyes seeming as honest as a child's.

"I think you should stay. Wait for your father. If I see anyone, I'll send them to you."

She twisted a diamond ring from her finger and held it out to him. "Take me with you."

He looked at the tiny circle of silver. "I don't wear silver."

"It's platinum."

"It's a bribe." She was used to buying what she wanted. He could see that. Buying her way out of what she could and letting Daddy clean up the rest. Had Daddy gotten tired of wiping up after her?

"Why not wait here?" she asked.

Tell her the truth, a partial truth or a lie? He looked down at her and lifted a hand to brush the soot from her cheek. The touch of her skin made his insides twitch as the longing rose again.

"Because I think the men who did this are close, and I think they want you or me dead."

Chapter Six

Meadow gaped, uncharacteristically finding herself rendered speechless. She had been around long enough to spot paranoia when she saw it. The guy said he'd been in Iraq. Maybe he had a screw or two loose.

Play along, she decided.

"What men? And why would they want us dead?"

"I don't know the answers to those questions. I do know that you and I being here exactly when that explosion went off is something more than coincidence."

"How could you possibly know that?"

Her savior did not answer. Instead, he gave her a long, uneasy look and turned away.

"Keep the shirt," he said. Then he lifted his camel pack and shrugged it onto his wide shoulders and started walking. With him went all the water they had.

"Hey, wait." She trotted to catch him, wishing her sandals were less cute and more practical. Wearing a wedge that showed her slim calves to best advantage seemed unnecessary when her legs were streaked with soot and covered with grit and sand. She caught him and grabbed at his arm, her hand covered with the long sleeve of his shirt. "Do you know how crazy you sound?"

He kept walking toward the road and the twisted remains of a bit of the blackened skeletal metal infrastructure that survived the blast. She let her gaze travel over the place where the eighteen-million-dollar home had been. She had not seen the explosion. The flash had been so bright and the earth had been shaking. He was right. It had been an explosion. What had caused the blast?

He was a firefighter, and even he had admitted that a gas tank could be the cause. But, as she looked at the ridgeline that she had been filming on and off for months, she realized the size of the demolition. It could not have been caused by a small propane tank or reserve tank for gas. She knew it in her heart.

Which meant someone had gone up there with explosives and set charges and pushed some kind of detonator and let the fires and rock spray down on the pine trees in the driest, hottest month of the year.

"Who would do this?"

He looked back. "You believe me now?"

She nodded. "It's just too big. I need to look at the footage. Maybe I can see something."

"I'd imagine the FBI will want to see that footage, as well."

"It's up on my feed. Anyone could have seen it live. But the entire thing, it's only recorded on this." She lifted the camera. "And on my server."

"Can't the social media sites recall it?"

"I don't know."

He started walking again.

She spotted a phone sticking out of his back pocket and jogged to come even with him again.

"You have a phone," she said, pointing at his pocket.

"No service," he said without slowing.

"You think you'll have service up there?" She pointed to the ridge.

"Maybe. I know Rustkin's got a well. Only water within ten miles. The fire started there and moved with the wind. Top of the ridge and the far side will be untouched."

She looked at the climb ahead of them. Meadow already felt dizzy, and the prospect of the hike made her stomach twist. Maybe she should wait for help. A glance back showed the billowing smoke off to the east. How long until anyone could drive out here. The road they were on dead-ended at the mansion that had once occupied the ridge. Emergency and Fire would concentrate on the threatened town of Pine View and the larger community of Valley View, which lay between the fire and Flagstaff. But her father. He'd come for her. He knew where she was.

When she glanced back to Dylan, it was to find him another two hundred feet along the road. The man was quick as a jackrabbit.

She stretched her legs and walked. By the time she drew even with him, her mouth felt like cotton.

"I need some water."

"No."

Now that was a word she didn't hear very often.

"Are you crazy? I'm thirsty."

"We don't have much left. We need to make it

up there first. Then, if I find the well, you can have a drink."

She stomped her foot, raising dust and his brow.

He was walking again. Meadow closed her dry mouth and lifted her stubborn chin. If he could make it up that mountain, then so could she.

SHE WAS TOUGHER than she looked, Dylan gave her that. The hike had to be four miles uphill, and she made it in those wedge sandals without another word of complaint or request for anything. In fact, it appeared that she would not even have taken the time of day from him if he had offered to give it to her.

Perhaps her strength was born of orneriness, but he still gave her credit for making the trek unassisted. He would have bet good money that she was going to start bawling like a branded calf or just stop so he'd have to bring water back to her.

Dylan glanced at the landscape surrounding them. He'd seen such a view before. Too often. The ground was scorched black and stank of charred wood. The fuel here had all been expended, the fire so hot that it had taken the crowns of every tree. The forest was gone, leaving denuded smoking trunks. The pristine view of the mountains, purchased at great expense, had now become bleak and ruined and would remain so for years to come.

Dylan lifted his phone and found a signal. He called Jack first, before his family and before his friend Ray, who was still a newlywed. He'd attended the ceremony in May. He knew now what no one but Ray and Morgan had known then. His new wife was already carrying his child. Seeing Ray happy for once, and settled with a wife and child, had been the deciding factor for Dylan. He wanted that. A wife. Children. And a job that didn't smell of charred trees and animals.

Jack picked up on the first ring, "Dylan!"

Dylan could tell from the echo on the connection that Jack was in his truck.

"Yes!"

"Where are you?"

Dylan gave him their position.

"Sit tight. I'm on my way."

It was over a 120 miles from Turquoise Canyon to Flagstaff and most of it on winding mountain roads.

Dylan told him he had a companion and relayed the name. Silence was his answer. Finally Jack spoke.

"Not good."

"Did you contact Kenshaw?" asked Dylan, inquiring about their shaman and the leader of Tribal Thunder, the warrior sect of Dylan's medicine society.

Jack said he had and that Kenshaw had been unable to reach Cheney Williams. "Kenshaw said he was there, right at the epicenter."

"What is the news saying?" asked Dylan.

"Forest fire. Evacuations. No mention of the explosion yet."

Dylan told him about the live streaming.

"I should be able to get that feed," said Jack. "Have to submit a request. If it captured a major crime, they'll release it."

Dylan scanned the smoking landscape. He'd call it major.

"Cheney Williams's death qualifies," said Jack. "Was the home owner up there?"

"I don't think so. Cheney said it would just be the two of us and a caretaker."

"I'll look into that. You have the caretaker's name?"

"No. Sorry. Maybe you ought to call Luke Forrest." Forrest was the field agent in charge when they took Jack's twin brother, Carter, into federal protection. Forrest was also Black Mountain Apache.

"Maybe. Hey, they've already called in our hotshots. Ray's heading up the guys in your absence. I guess you won't be crew captain on this one."

The Turquoise Canyon Hotshots were going on assignment without him. That was what he had wanted, wasn't it? The reason he'd gone back for training as a fire-safety inspector. So why did his gut ache?

"Yeah."

"I can't get to you until the fire is off the road. You got water?"

"Soon."

"All right, Brother Bobcat. Hold on. I've got another call. It's Forrest."

Dylan heard a double beep indicating he was on hold. He disconnected and continued along. They needed water.

"So, Cheney was here?" asked Meadow. It was the first she'd spoken to him in over an hour.

"Yeah. I'm sorry. He's gone." Now Dylan was wondering if Williams was a victim or some sort of suicide bomber. Kenshaw had recommended Dylan for this job, but now Dylan wondered exactly how his shaman knew this attorney who had lived down here in the valley? And why hadn't Cheney sent one of his staff to meet Dylan up here on the ridge? If he worked with Meadow's father, he must have people to do such things.

"Why did he call you brother bobcat?" she asked.

"You could hear that?"

She nodded.

"Bobcat is my spirit animal." He pushed up the sleeve of his T-shirt, showing her the tattoo. "This is his track."

She stroked a finger over the muscle of his arm and purred, her hand lingering. Dylan's muscles twitched as he grappled with the tension now overtaking him.

He stepped back, breaking the connection between them.

She distracted him. Made it hard for him to think. Now the questions swarmed him again. Buzzing around his head like gnats when he reached the crest of the ridge. Nothing of the building had survived. The explosion had ripped away the rock beneath the building. The infinity edge pool that had floated above the valley on steel legs, the house, garage and guest suite—all gone.

Dylan checked his phone for calls and found the battery dangerously low. "I'm almost out of juice."

"Switch it off and then check it periodically."

"Will do."

Dylan made another call to his parents' home and reached his grandfather, Frank. He told him quickly what had happened, and that he was safe and Jack Bear Den was coming to get him. He remembered to tell the old man that he loved him before he disconnected. Frank Florez was the only father Dylan had ever known.

When he finished, he turned off his phone.

"That was sweet. Your father?" she asked.

"Yes, but officially he's my grandfather. My mother's father."

"What clan?" she asked.

"Butterfly."

"Same as your mother, of course."

Dylan could see how Meadow had gotten all A's in school. She was quick.

"Can I call my family?" she asked.

That was a bad idea. Her dad would find out she had survived eventually from his radio communication. But he didn't want her father knowing exactly where to find them.

"Not yet."

She lifted a brow but said nothing, keeping her thoughts to herself as they continued up the hill.

He moved farther up and over the ridge. He had left the road to climb past the wreckage and so had not seen beyond the epicenter of the blaze to the pristine pavers of the curving drive that led to the untouched gate and gatehouse beyond the flashpoint of the fire. His mouth quirked in a smile.

Meadow arrived beside him a moment later. Her face was dangerously red. He gave her the mouthpiece to the camel pack and she took a long drink. Then he led them to the gatehouse. The only standing structure had survived the blast by being well down the private road and back from the ridge. The fire had spared the gatehouse only because prevailing winds had carried the blaze in the opposite direction, westward from the epicenter of the blast.

The Rustkin gatehouse was larger than his home on the rez. Dylan knocked on the front door but received no answer.

"You said on the phone the guy would be here," said Meadow.

"That's what Cheney told me." Dylan tried again, knocking louder. Then they gave up and circled the home. He broke a window in the garage and crawled inside, then disconnected the opener and hauled up the door himself. Meadow stepped inside.

"Phew," she said. "Cool in here." She glanced around. "No cars."

Dylan hoped the caretaker was far away because the road that circled down the unscathed side of the mountain met the burning side at the break in the ridgeline. If the caretaker had evacuated, he would not get far.

She cupped her hands to her mouth and shouted a hello. There was no reply. She turned to Dylan. "Well, we have lights and AC."

"Generator out back. Saw it on the way in."

"Let's take a look around," she said.

She was a bold one, he'd give her that—perhaps a little too daring. Dylan didn't just charge forward. He was more of a planner.

"Maybe you should wait here."

"Hell with that."

Meadow pivoted and led the way down the hall and past the office facing the drive, through the small living space and into the kitchen in the back.

There she stuck her entire head under the sink faucet and soaked her hair making the blue and purple turn a darker shade. Then she drank until he thought her stomach might rupture.

When she drew back, she whipped her head up so that the ends sent a spray of water to the ceiling.

"How do you feel?" he asked.

"Alive, thanks to you. But I'm dizzy…and what a headache."

"Heat exhaustion." Or heat stroke, he thought.

"Never had it this bad." She stepped aside and Dylan drank. Then he soaked his head, letting the lukewarm water wash away the sweat and sand from his short hair. The water was heaven.

"I'm going to find a bathroom. I need a shower."

"I'll check the generator."

She cast him a glance over one shoulder and shrugged. "Suit yourself."

Had she been inviting him along? That idea should have sent him in the opposite direction because he did not want to listen to the water running while he imagined Meadow washing her tempting body clean. Instead, he watched her walk away.

She strode down the hall that presumably led to the bedroom and bath. On the way she dropped the shirt he had lent her, giving him an unforgettable view of her back broken only by the lace bra. He'd kept her from being burned. Every inch of her was perfect, if dirty. Her tan covered her skin all the way to her bottom, which seemed very white by comparison above the scrap of pink lace. She cast a final glance over her shoulder and gave him a wink.

"You're up next." She reached behind her back and unfastened the bra as she turned, heedless of the glimpse she gave him of her body in profile. She was smaller up top than he had imagined, small and round and perfect. Thanks to him.

Dylan found the generator ran on propane and had switched on automatically when the power quit. How long it would last was just a guess, but he thought this would be the place to bed down tonight. Still, he would be careful about what electricity they used. He did a perimeter check familiarizing himself with his surroundings, then returned to the house and checked the rooms. The kitchen had a small table and chairs, and both the living room and the single bedroom were furnished. Someone had been living here, judging from the books, laptop and half-full coffeepot. The mail on the counter was addressed to David Kaneda. Dylan used his camera to snap a shot and sent it to Jack Bear Den with the message that they had reached the caretaker's house, which was empty. Jack's replay was the letter K.

Okay.

He busied himself filling his camel pack and then checking the landline, which was dead. The security system was not yet functioning, though the metal gate across the drive was locked. Unfortunately, the wall was not finished and a temporary road had been graded beyond the gate for construction vehicles to complete one of the most expensive homes in Arizona—and the only one that broke the ridge. Was that why they had blown it up?

They'd achieved a two-for-one, endangering the affluent community in the valley, as well.

He searched the cupboards and refrigerator. The refrigerator had bottled water, some of those sixty-four-ounce soda-fountain drinks and leftovers from lunches, some fruit, two half sandwiches—one meatball and one roast beef that smelled edible. On the counter he found chips.

Dylan arranged some of the food on the kitchen table and listened but did not hear the water running.

"You done?" he called.

"I didn't start yet."

"Why?"

"No soap."

Meadow called from the shower. "Is there soap out there?"

He searched and came up with a bottle of liquid hand soap and was halfway down the hall when he paused as all kinds of erotic images flooded him.

Dylan debated his options. Sex meant nothing to her. He patted his front pocket where his wallet held two condoms. He had principles, but he was still a man.

"Dylan?"

"I found some."

He stepped into the steaming air of the bathroom. The glass door gave him a pretty fair image of what she looked like naked and wet. He growled and lifted the soap over the top of the glass barrier.

"There are no towels," she said, accepting the soap and then tipping her head back to let the spray of water cascade over her crown.

"They're in the linen closet in the hall."

She rolled back the shower door. He didn't look away.

"So, do we have a bed?" she asked. She was so casual about her body and sexuality. *Do we have a bed?*

"There's only one."

"That'll do."

Now his skin was prickling and his body responding to the possibilities she raised.

"Is that all you ever have on your mind?" he asked.

She faced him, pressing herself against the glass, giving him a view he would never forget. "Only since I met you."

He didn't believe it, but he found himself growing hard.

"Why don't you step in? I'll wash you off."

"Meadow, I don't even know you."

"You will if you get in here."

Dylan untied his boots and stripped out of his clothing. He retrieved his wallet and one condom. Then he ignored his conscience, slid back the door and stepped into the shower with Meadow.

Chapter Seven

"Man," she said, her smile widening. "You are fine to look at."

"You sure about this?" His body pulsed with need.

"Totally."

He'd never slept with someone who said *totally*. It wasn't right. Dylan dropped the condom onto the tiled shelf and closed the shower door.

"I thought I had burned my back in the shelter." He presented it to her. "But I don't feel any burns."

Her hands caressed his shoulders as the water pulsed on his skin.

"Perfect," she said. She soaped him and lathered his skin from his neck to the back of his legs while his body built to a thrumming need to touch her.

Meadow's hand slipped down his arm pausing at the tattoo.

"I like this. It's well done. That's a medicine shield. Right? And eagle feathers?"

He nodded, watching her as she traced the design.

She slipped around in front of him and repeated her ministration on his chest.

"I've wanted to touch you since I saw you with

that ax. Then you were on top of me and I could barely breathe."

"I'm sorry about that."

"Don't be."

"It's a one-person shelter. We might be the first to ever share one."

Her hands stilled on his chest.

"Dylan, I know you said you don't…you know. But I really like you."

"That why you wouldn't speak to me?"

"That was childish. I was so hot and thirsty." She lifted up on her toes and kissed his cheek. He tilted his head and kissed her back, their mouths melting and tongues dancing.

What was he doing? She was trouble. This was Theron Wrangler's youngest daughter. Chances were good that she was involved in this. Maybe he could find out.

It was an excuse to have her—and a thin one at that—but he took it. He broke the kiss and turned her so that her perfect white bottom molded to his hips. His erection slid between her legs and she pushed back.

"What is it you want, Meadow?"

"Isn't that obvious?"

He cupped her breasts, toying with her nipples, pinching until her head fell back against his chest and she cried out in excitement. Then he stroked her stomach, thighs, the inside of her thighs. She opened her legs and he flicked a thumb over the tiny bud of pleasure. Meadow rubbed back against him, making it hard to concentrate.

"Why were you here, Meadow?" he whispered. "Why today?"

"Bad timing," she answered.

"Whose idea was it, this filming of the construction?"

She gasped and braced her hands on the tile, giving him more pressure as she pushed back, her slippery thighs caressing his erection. He closed his eyes and tilted his head back.

"Who?" he repeated.

"My father. He said I'd be doing him a favor."

"What favor?"

"A fast-motion montage of the home breaking the ridge, spoiling the natural beauty of the mountains."

And a fast-motion view of it tumbling down again.

"He sent you today?"

She nodded, her vocalizations now tiny cries.

And Kenshaw had sent him today.

"No more talk," she said, and rubbed against him. His fingers glided over slick flesh and she trembled.

Meadow's cries grew louder and her body jerked as her pleasure took her. Dylan held her as she turned into his arms, pressing her cheek to his chest. She fit just perfectly against him, and for a moment he wished she was someone else, someone he could keep.

"You're good," she whispered.

She reached between them, grasping him with experienced hands. Dylan knew he should step away. He tried, but it only gave her better leverage. Her clever fingers and water all worked against his best intentions. She stroked and his body hummed with the building need.

"We'll save the condom for later," she said. "How's that?"

She glided against him, trapping his erection between her soft stomach and her hands. His head fell back and he knew he was lost.

He didn't last long and had to brace his arms against the glass and tile to keep his knees from giving way. The truth was that he'd felt something with Meadow that was unfamiliar...longing. He admitted to himself that he wanted her. Wanted all of her. Wanted to stretch her out on that bed and slowly explore every inch. He wanted to take her to see the sunset over Turquoise Lake and to see the spot where he dug out the best turquoise from the vein deep in the heart of his reservation and the vein of the sacred blue stone that threaded through the canyon along the river.

But he admitted what this was for her—just a quick, meaningless encounter or, worse, a thank-you. Her hands fell away and the emptiness yawned inside him.

She smiled up at him. "You always talk so much?"

He shook his head. "Not usually."

"You're no expert interrogator, that's for sure. You should sneak up on things. Not just jump right at it." She lifted the bottle of hand soap. "Want me to wash your hair?" she asked.

Dylan sighed. He'd been too overt again. "No. Meadow. I'll do it. What you said before, was that all true?"

"I have no reason to lie, though I'm super good at it. Ask me something personal?"

"Have you done this before?"

Her eyes went wide. "Never. You're my first."

A shot of regret pierced him. She'd led him to believe she was experienced.

"I'm sorry. We shouldn't have…"

"Oh, relax. I was lying. I'd better get out." She handed over the soap.

"You're very casual about sex," he said.

She pressed a hand to her hip. "That wasn't sex, Dylan. That was a hand job. If we have sex, you'll see the difference."

He made a strangled sound that was his best attempt at a laugh.

She let her hand slide back to her side. "I'm starving. Find anything to eat?"

"In the kitchen."

She strode naked and dripping out the door. *Brazen*, his mother would say. Uninhibited, he thought. Did it bother him that she was experienced?

Double standard if it did, he thought. But he found himself unsettled by the encounter. It wasn't until the suds were streaming over his face and chest that he realized why. It wasn't that she had had other men— it was that he didn't want her to have any more. Except him.

"That's crazy," he said, and rinsed. "You have as much chance of keeping her as catching wildfire."

He shut off the water, using his hands like the blade of a squeegee to shuck off the excess water. He shook his head, sending droplets flying. He was only damp when he stepped onto the tile floor and reached for his jeans. The smell of smoke hit him instantly, but there was no help for it.

Meadow returned with a towel cinched about her hips. She extended a second one to him.

When he reached the hall, it was to find Meadow standing half-naked in the corridor beside the open accordion doors. Inside the closet sat a stacked laundry and shelving with clean linens and bath towels. She tossed her bra and panties into the washer leaving herself naked.

He lifted the shirt so it draped on his index finger.

"Looking for this?" he asked.

"It stinks. Throw it in here." She stepped aside.

"Do you do everything naked?" he asked.

"Only the important things." She shot him a blazing smile full of perfectly straightened white teeth. She collected the rest of his clothing and tossed them into the washer.

"My dad could send a helicopter for us. Want me to call him?" she asked.

Dylan hadn't thought of that. Her family would be worried sick.

His gut told him no, but how could he deny her?

"Too dangerous," he lied. In fact, it would be safe to approach by helicopter from the east, skirting the plume of smoke. Dylan looked away.

She returned to washing his shirt.

"To land here or to trust my dad?"

He didn't answer.

She added the soap and started the machine.

"My father did not send me up here to get caught in that wildfire. So you are going to need another theory."

He said nothing.

"We were closest to the explosion. You filmed it and I was up there, or nearly." He would have been if she had not delayed him. Had she done that on purpose, knowing what would come?

He rubbed his neck and tried to decide what to believe.

"The police will want to speak to us," he said, and waited for her reaction.

She closed the washer door. "Fine. I've got nothing to hide."

Truth or lie? he wondered.

His friend Jack had suspicions that Kenshaw was using Tribal Thunder for his own purposes. He told Dylan he believed Kenshaw had sent Carter down there to rescue his niece because he had foreknowledge of the Lilac shooting. Then their shaman had arranged for Ray to protect Morgan before the FBI even knew that BEAR was targeting her for fear Morgan knew who had hired her dad. Dylan had been there with Morgan and Ray when two masked members of BEAR had shown up and told Morgan that they had determined she knew nothing. Now here he was with Meadow the day the ridge house exploded.

"I don't mind police. But the tabloids. Oh, man. Get ready, because you are about to get famous."

He didn't like the sound of that. He was not shy but would describe himself as a private person.

"My savior." She started the machine. "Don't

worry. I won't tell them about our communal shower if you don't. Or that we slept together."

"We haven't…"

She smiled. "Day's not over yet."

He'd never met a woman so blasé about filling her sexual needs. Did she want him or would anyone do?

She glanced out the window. "Let that run while we get something to eat." She headed down the hall, releasing her towel and fixing it again under her armpits.

He stepped into the bedroom and retrieved his phone. He flicked it on and called Jack.

"You okay?" asked Jack.

"So far."

"Where are you?"

Dylan told him.

"Good spot. Listen. I spoke with Forrest. That video feed has gone viral. Ms. Wrangler caught the exact moment the hillside blew. Plus, because of your radio distress call, they know you both survived. Local law enforcement is calling the fire suspicious."

"That was quick. They haven't investigated."

"Dylan, the news is reporting that sources say you are wanted in connection. Both of you. So you're a suspect. One news program is speculating that you are one of those guys who starts a fire and then puts it out."

"Hero complex," said Dylan. He sure had the right background for that.

"Luke says it stinks. He wants you out of there before the locals take you."

"How do we do that?"

"That's the problem. All access is blocked by the

fire. He's trying to get a helicopter. Agent Forrest told me he's got his doubts that if you are arrested, that you two will make it to a station. He's afraid the plan was to pin the whole thing on you two all along."

"Whose plan?" he asked.

"Forrest thinks it's BEAR because they have the explosives."

"If they match," said Dylan.

"Takes time to determine that. Time we don't have."

"Could it be her father?"

"Forrest mentioned that. He's the logical suspect. Already linked to the Lilac mine shooting. You think Meadow is involved?"

"I'm not sure. My impression is that her being here is her father's doing. She thinks she's working on a documentary film about the house that broke the ridgeline."

"What do you think?"

"I think her dad sent her here to die. Make her a martyr for BEAR's causes."

"You don't have to convince me or Forrest. You have to convince the police if they get to you first."

"They won't. What about Kurt and the air ambulance?" asked Dylan. Jack's little brother was a paramedic out of Darabee.

"They're evacuating the firefighters on the line. Heat illness. It was a hundred and three out there. You got water?"

"Yes. How's the fire?"

"Twenty percent contained." Jack gave him the details. "No one is getting in to you. Road is closed. Your crew is out there."

Without him. That was the first time he hadn't been with them. Twelve men working the line.

"Is Ray there?"

"Yes, he's the one who told me you should stay put."

That gave Dylan some ease, but the guilt was still there. The silence stretched. Dylan pressed a hand to his forehead.

"Listen. You can't be there, so forget it."

Jack was right.

"Did you find a phone charger?"

"Not yet."

"Okay. Concentrate on what you can do."

"What's that?"

"Don't get caught. Tomorrow, maybe you can try to jump the fire line and rejoin your crew."

"What about Meadow?"

"You need to get as far away from that one as possible."

Chapter Eight

Jack thought Meadow was involved. Even if she wasn't, Dylan's friend believed that her father was responsible for the fire. He said his instinct told him that the blast was caused by explosives stolen from the Lilac Copper Mine.

Meadow didn't seem like an eco-extremist to Dylan but, really, they were strangers. His mind replayed their encounter in the shower and he groaned. He switched the phone off to preserve the battery that was now in the red. If he could find a charger he'd be all set.

He searched the bedroom and came up empty. He found Meadow in the kitchen and searched again for a charger but with no luck.

"I found a pantry." She showed him the locked door she had shimmied open.

Dylan was going to tell her that was stealing, but emergencies required allowances. The food was cans and boxes, but the pork and beans and peas tasted better than anything in his memory. He tried to tell himself it was his hunger, but he knew it was Meadow. Truth be told, he enjoyed her company. She told him about being sent off to boarding school at ten. Even though she kept the stories limited to the predicaments she had found herself in and even though he laughed, because she was such an expert at telling a story, he kept wondering why she had been sent away.

Finally the meal was done, and still they sat across from each other, wrapped in clean towels and sharing stories. He told her about Iraq and how he'd lost one of his best friends to insurgents. How his friend had been tortured and finally killed. It was a story he didn't share. He also told her about his dad, who had left his family when Dylan was seven. Dylan had not been the oldest but he had taken charge. His brother Danny had taken off at seventeen for the rodeo circuit. He told her how his younger brother, Donny, now danced professionally at powwows for prize money. "Even danced in DC at the American Indian museum they got there," he added.

"They both left you holding the bag."

"I was in the service for four years. But, yeah, when I got home, Donny left, too. He comes home from time to time. Mom and Gramps make his regalia. Sometimes he brings money." Most times Donny needed it, Dylan thought.

"That's why you were so good. Your mom needed you," she said. Then she sniffed. "Mine never did."

"Did your brothers and sisters all go to boarding school, too?"

Her smile dropped. He had a moment to see behind the fun-loving facade to the pain she hid beneath.

"Only me."

"Because you were so much younger?" Perhaps

they just had not wanted to deal with a teen when all her siblings were grown.

"My mother's idea. She said I lacked discipline. The girls' version of military school."

"Had you been in trouble?"

She glanced away. "Not yet. That came after they sent me off. Back then I was Daddy's little girl. My mom said I was too needy and, well, nothing I did really pleased her."

How terrible, he thought.

"So why did you get into so much trouble at school?"

She looked at him as if he were dim. Then she forced a smile. "Just growing up, you know, testing the limits."

Then it struck him and he understood. "When you tested the limits, they sent you home."

She met his gaze and he knew he was right.

"For a while," she said.

"You ever get in trouble at home?"

She shook her head. "Am I that easy to read?"

"No, but it's funny. I've always been a source of pride for my family—but not because I always wanted to do what was right. I'm not a Boy Scout, despite what you think. I just never wanted to see the disappointment on my mother's face. Maybe that doesn't make me brave. There were times I wanted to do what I liked, take what I wanted."

She gave him a look charged with desire, and he felt his longing build.

"Take what exactly?" she whispered.

His breathing quickened, but he did not say that what he wanted right now was her.

"You can take me, Dylan. No one needs to know that the Eagle Scout stumbled. I'll never tell."

He believed her and he stood to go to her. He knelt beside her and stroked the petal-soft skin of her cheek all the way down her throat to the top of her chest, feeling the swell of her breast above the rolled top of the bath towel.

"I wish I could," he said.

She pressed her forehead to his and closed her eyes. "You can."

He drew back. "I don't just want sex, Meadow. I want a woman who will stand by me. One who understands me and who loves me. You and I, we'll be going in different directions soon."

She took his hand and laced her fingers to his. "I could stick around."

Now he smiled at the ridiculousness of that image. "You gonna move onto the rez? Raise cattle? Maybe you could work in the cultural center or up at the ruins touring visitors. No, you aren't sticking around, Meadow. You aren't the type. You know it and I know it."

"No one ever asked me to stick around." Something in her tone made it seem to Dylan as if she really wanted him to ask. But he couldn't. He barely knew her and it wouldn't work. They were too different.

"You need to get back to your world," he said, and stood.

She lifted her chin and smiled. The mask returned to its place. The fun-loving party girl was back.

"Whatever you say. So who gets the bed?"

MEN DID NOT turn her down, Meadow thought. That made Dylan a challenge. She hated being rejected. But, if she were honest with herself, and she very rarely was, this man was different. He had a purpose and a depth of character that she admired. She even admired that he wouldn't sleep with her.

Refreshing. But his reticence had backfired and now she wanted more than sex. He intrigued her. With Dylan she glimpsed a different way, and somehow she wanted to earn his respect. Trouble was, she had no idea how to begin. He didn't respect her and why would he?

Meadow checked the washer and loaded the clean, wet clothing into the dryer. When she returned to the kitchen, she found that Dylan had cleared her place and was washing dishes. She found a towel and dried. The dryer buzzer sounded and she traded her towel for her under things and Dylan's clean fire-resistant shirt, while Dylan drew on his jeans and shrugged into his T-shirt. In the caretaker's closet he found her a pair of gym shorts, but she rejected them. His shirt was covering enough, and if she couldn't get close to him, she could be close to his things. She lifted the collar to her nose and inhaled the smell of soap, but not the man whom the garment belonged.

"It's clean," he said.

"Too bad," she replied.

He cast her that look, the one that mingled caution with intrigue.

They sat for a time in the kitchen and he shared with her tales of firefighting and soldiering and what it was like to be a boy who rode his horse to school.

When she suppressed a yawn, he called a halt and took her off to bed.

"You're sleeping here, too," she insisted.

"That's a bad idea."

"It's the only bed," she said. "And if you're such a paragon of virtue, you should be able to ignore little old me for a few hours."

"I have a feeling no one ignores you, Meadow." He gave her a smile.

"My mother does." She had meant it to be a flippant remark, but the truth of her words stuck in her throat and her next breath was a strangled thing.

His smile drooped and he stroked her cheek. Mothers were supposed to love their children unconditionally, weren't they?

The tears came next and Dylan gathered her up, tucking her head under his chin.

"She avoids me unless I'm in trouble."

"So, you're in trouble a lot."

"Yup. Then my dad swoops in and fixes things and I get to see him and everything is good, you know, although he's disappointed. Then my mom gets a hold of me." Meadow shook her head. "It's like she can't wait to see me leave. I've tried everything. She just hates me."

He stroked her back. "I'm sure that's not so. Maybe she is just worried about you."

"And disappointed. But when I do well, she's just as dissatisfied. Worse, actually."

"How do you mean?"

"I got all good grades at my first prep school, hoping I could come home if I did well. She said that my dad was a generous donor, so the teachers wouldn't dare fail me. Dylan, I earned those grades, but she just…" Meadow inhaled and then blew away the breath. "Once my dad had me working as an assistant on his documentary on the reintroduction of wolves in Wyoming. He said my filming was really good and so he was taking me on location with him. She threw a fit about how he handed me everything and I needed to make my own way. So he didn't take me."

"You need to do what is right for yourself, Meadow. Not for your mother or your father."

"Really? You don't know my family. My oldest sister, Connie, is an aid worker in Uganda. You know my oldest brother, Phillip, is CEO of PAN, Protecting All Nature. Next brother, Miguel, he's a pediatrician with Doctors Without Borders. My sister Rosalie oversees PAN's projects, all of them, including reintroducing wolves into their natural habitat. My other sister, Katrina, does pro bono work for convicts and helps with marketing campaigns for my father's documentaries. We've got a CEO, two doctors, two attorneys and then there is me."

"You could be any of those things."

"It won't make any difference. If you're right, they sent me out here like Gretel to get lost in the forest and be eaten by the witch."

That he could not deny, because he believed it.

He continued to rub her back. "On Turquoise Canyon we have strong traditions and a rich heritage. We also have poverty, substance abuse and one of the shortest life expectancies in the nation. Forty-eight.

That's the average for a man who stays there. It's why my brothers left and why I left."

"You don't have sisters?"

"I do. Two of them. Both older. Rita and Gianna married young. They have kids. They never left the rez. But I joined the Marines. I learned things, saw things, and I am a different man than the one I might have been—but I am still Apache. So I returned to my people and joined a medicine society. I swore to protect my tribe and keep my body strong."

"Eagle Scout."

"Bobcat, remember?"

She smiled and pressed her face against the warmth of his muscular chest. If only she could just stay here in his arms.

"You make your parents proud."

He didn't answer.

"Dylan?"

"My mom is proud. Dad took off when I was a kid, right after Donny was born. You want to make your dad proud while I want to be nothing like mine. I want to be there for my children and teach them what it is to walk in beauty."

"Walk in beauty?"

"It is a way to live that is in balance with the natural world."

"My father would approve of that."

The conversation lulled, but still she felt at ease. It didn't seem necessary to fill the silences.

"Do you think you could just hold me awhile tonight?"

His silence stretched, and she felt needy and weak.

"Sure. Yes, I can do that."

Likely he could. She couldn't think of a single man she had ever known who would have said yes to that and then not used it as a way to get into her panties. But Dylan meant he could do it and he would. She didn't know if that should make her happy or bereft. A little of both, she supposed.

"Thank you."

He tucked her in and lay on top of the coverlet, one big strong arm wrapped around her shoulders. She laid a hand on his ribbed stomach and felt his muscles twitch through the thin cotton. Meadow smiled and released a sigh. The skin of his bare arms turned to gooseflesh. The temptation to stroke him was strong but she resisted. Gradually he relaxed and she did, as well. When was the last time she had lain beside a man like this?

Never. A first, and that was rare enough. And to her surprise she discovered that she had missed a kind of intimacy that went beyond sex. She was at ease with Dylan. She trusted him enough to let him see what others did not—her pain.

His breathing softened. His mouth gaped and she smiled. The night could not be long enough for her. She did not dream, but woke as the bright morning sunlight stole across her face.

Why hadn't they thought to close the blinds?

Sometime during the night she had rolled to her side and Dylan had rolled with her. He now spooned against her. Her bottom was pressed against his groin and, although she could tell from his breathing that he still slept, she could feel a spectacular erection. He had one arm around her and across her chest so that his hand held her shoulder as if he was a lifeguard preparing to tow her to safety. She smiled and stretched, rubbing her bottom against him.

His breathing stopped and his body tensed.

"Good morning," she said, looking back at him.

He released her and rolled to his back. She rolled with him, draping a hand over his chest. He blew away a breath.

"Sorry," he said.

"Mornings. It happens. Right?"

"Yeah." He pinched his eyes closed and pressed his forearm over his eyes. "You are such a temptation, Meadow."

She wanted to be. But she also felt anxious because she did not just want to sleep with him. She wanted...more.

Oh, boy. She was in trouble again.

Chapter Nine

Dylan needed a moment to compose himself. It had been a long time since he had lain beside a woman all night and never when he had not slept with her. His gaze fell on Meadow as the dawn crept over the sky, painting her skin pink and lavender. She was nothing like any of the others.

His three serious relationships had all ended badly when each woman expressed her wish for marriage, forcing Dylan to face the hard fact that he was not in love with any of them. Margarete had said he was afraid of commitment because his father had left them. But the commitment-phobic didn't sign enlistment papers, did they? Maybe it wasn't the same thing. He had decided long ago that if female company came at the cost of a marriage, he would not settle until he fell in love. He wanted kids but not badly enough to pick just anyone. So far, he had not been lucky enough to find a woman with whom he could imagine wishing to spend his life.

He had watched Meadow in the rising light as she slept and wondered at the strange feelings of intimacy. Before she had fallen into sleep had been the most difficult, his intentions to comfort battling with his need to possess. He blamed it on the fire. Ever since he had taken her into his shelter, he'd felt an overwhelming need to protect her.

Meadow slipped to the edge of the bed they had shared, just like newlyweds. Well, he admitted, nothing like newlyweds. If that had been their wedding night, he most certainly would not have stopped at a few kisses. Still, having her cuddle up to him in the night had broken loose something inside him and now he wanted…what? A date? Too late for that. A relationship? He imagined how his brothers in Tribal Thunder would laugh at that. He knew of no couple who were such a mismatch, unless it was Anglo Cassidy Walker Cosen and her husband, Clyne. She had married one of the tribal councilmen on Black Mountain, much to the consternation of many in his tribe. If he had done it…

But this woman was a little crazy and he liked that. Was surprised he liked it.

Meadow murmured, and when her eyelids fluttered open, their gazes locked.

"You all right?" she asked, and rolled toward him, placing a hand at his opposite hip. "You haven't changed your mind?"

He tried to keep his attention on her pretty, sleepy face, but his gaze dipped to slide down her body. Meadow had kicked off most of the covers during the night, revealing smooth, tight skin interrupted only by her pink bra and panties.

"About?"

"You know." She ran a finger down the center of

his chest and paused where the sheets covered his pulsing erection.

He swallowed, trying to think with the rational part of his brain and not the animal part that roared to take what she offered.

"Meadow, you don't think this can go anywhere, right?" Had he sounded hopeful? *Please, no.*

"I think it can go any number of interesting places."

"What I mean is—do you want me just for this?" He motioned at the evidence of his preparedness.

Her gaze trailed down him, and he swore he could feel her attention like a caress.

"I don't know why you'd want anything else. No one else does. At first, men want sex or an introduction to my parents. Some latch on to me in hopes I might actually come into serious money someday. Those are the worst."

"I don't want those things."

She sighed. "Pity. Especially about the sex. I'd know how to handle you then." She allowed her hand to trail up his thigh, letting him know exactly what she intended to handle.

"I want to protect you, Meadow. That means keeping you from starting something that isn't going to work out."

Her hand splayed on his thigh. "It might."

He met her gaze and saw, reflected in her warm eyes, the need for a connection that matched his own. He sat up.

"No one will let us be," he said, still trying to be the voice of reason. "My mom, my friends, my tribe."

"My parents, friends and family would be shocked. But I'm not sure they'd be disappointed."

"But shocked," he echoed.

"That I finally picked a man of character. Sure would."

He switched to the language of his birth as he stroked her cheek. "I wish it could be you."

"What does that mean?"

"We don't have time."

The disappointment made him ache.

"Oh, right." She reached to the end table and handed him his phone. "You better check in. See if we can get through."

He booted up the phone, which now showed a red bar over his voice message page. The battery was nearly empty. Jack had left him a message. Ray Strong, too. Both were unread, but he never left his phone on the voice mail page.

She slipped to the edge of the bed and headed toward the bathroom. He wondered if Meadow had used his phone. He'd never set the password protection. She'd had an opportunity to use his phone when he'd been in the shower. He glanced from the phone to the hallway where she had disappeared.

Again he wondered if he was sleeping with the enemy.

He checked the recent calls but found nothing. She could have deleted it. Then he checked his two messages. He listened to Ray's first and discovered where the fire was contained and where his crew was working. Jack's message was next and he listened as she reappeared and sat on his side at the foot of the bed.

"The road is opening at eight a.m. State police said they'll let the home owners through at around ten. Anyone could be heading at you. Pick up, Dylan. Listen. If you are at the gatehouse, you need to get out of there."

Dylan glanced at the phone's screen and saw it was only a few minutes after eight. He was up and dressed in moments. Unfortunately, Meadow still wore only her underwear.

He explained that someone was coming.

"That's good. Isn't it?"

"Not necessarily. We should be out of here before they arrive, just in case."

"In case of what?"

He explained it to her as Meadow slipped into her sandals.

"Find some clothing. Look in his dresser," he said motioning to the chest of drawers presumably belonging to the gatekeeper.

"They can't think we started this. It's ridiculous."

Dylan's people had been on the receiving end of many injustices. Unlike Meadow, he did not expect to get fair treatment.

"We have to go," said Dylan.

"I'm not going back out there."

"Wait here, then," he said.

"Maybe I think I will." That stubborn chin lifted again.

Dylan glanced out the window that showed the road that wound up to the gatehouse. That was when he spotted a rooster tail of dust. They were already here.

"It's a bad idea."

She followed the direction of his gaze.

"Cavalry has arrived?"

Looked more like trouble to Dylan. All his internal alarms were sounding.

He lifted his brows. "You realize the cavalry used to shoot my people on sight, don't you?"

"If you're planning on hiding, you better scoot before they get here," she said.

He grabbed her wrist. "Come with me."

She shook him off and he let her go. She thumbed toward the kitchen window. "Listen. I appreciate everything you did for me, but I am not going out there again unless there is air-conditioning." She lifted to her toes to peer out the window as Dylan ducked out of sight. "There, at the gate. Oh, a Hummer!"

It was, indeed. Not the commercial kind sold to posers in the cities but a Humvee that had armor plating. He had been in one when Hatch Yeager had been killed that night when they'd been ordered to secure the road. This vehicle was close to a mobile tank that could move across the desert or through the woods as long as there was a gap big enough in the trees. It also did not show any signs of having traveled through the fire.

There was only one road leading to this home to Pine View and between here and there the fire still raged. The road to from Valley View, through Pine Valley and then began hitched back and forth up the ridge, until the incline became too steep. The road then threaded between the ridges to continue up the gentler slope behind the mountain. This made practical sense and afforded an impressive view of the controversial home on approach. If the Humvee had driven over the valley road and through the wildfire, there would have been evidence, ash covering the surface, possibly pink fire retardant around the wheel wells or charring of the exterior paint. But there was none of that.

Dylan made the next logical conclusion. They had been inside the perimeter of fire. In other words, they had traveled down behind the ridge but never crossed into the valley of devastation beyond. So whoever was in that vehicle, they had been here since before the fire.

"Meadow. Listen, we have to go now. Those aren't friends."

"Dylan, I'm not going out there to scramble over those rocks again. My feet are blistered. Forget it."

The construction route remained open, leaving the security gate blocking an unfinished road. Even if theh perimeter was operational, that Humvee would blast right through it.

Meadow stepped past him. Dylan waited by the side door, slipping out as the Humvee roared through the missing section of wall and onto the flat, paved road beyond. It stopped in front of the main entrance as he crept around the back of the gatehouse, so he was there when the driver in combat boots stepped down from the vehicle. Dylan's eyes narrowed, knowing at a glance that this was not the home owner. The driver was dressed in desert camouflage, but the familiar name patch, black-and-white US flag and service insignia were missing. In other words, there was nothing to identify him. His designer mirror Oakleys were not regulation. His red hair was short but not buzzed, and his build was athletic. His stride contained a swagger of a young man.

His copilot emerged from the opposite side, similarly dressed with no soot or ash on his clothing. He was in his middle years, already well into the third quadrant of the medicine wheel. His hair was buzzed perhaps to hide the hairline that had receded back to his bald spot. He slipped on a cap with a brim that shaded his pale eyes. This one had the look of ex-military, right down to his crisp walk.

"Let's get this over with," said the passenger, who seemed to be the man in charge.

Dylan locked his jaw. *Get what over with?* He called on Bobcat to help him see what they intended and to be patient as he waited for his chance.

"I'm shooting him if he makes a move," said the young one.

"We don't even know if he's here."

"Survived the fire, though," said Red.

His commander searched the ground and quickly found the tracks that marked Dylan and Meadow's arrival.

"They said he's an ex-marine," said the young one, drawing his personal weapon and looking about as if Dylan would spring at him from behind the ornamental boulders that lined the drive.

There was no such thing as an ex-marine. Or that's what his sergeant had told him. Once a marine, always a marine. *Semper fi.*

"Put that away," ordered the one in command. "As far as anyone knows, they didn't leave the shelter.

No radio contact from him since the distress call at twelve-hundred hours yesterday."

Dylan darted from the house to the grill of the Hummer, reaching the driver's side as the older man knocked on the gatehouse door like a service call instead of what Dylan judged him to be—a killer on a cleanup mission.

He heard them speaking as they approached the gatehouse. Dylan slipped the passenger door open and searched the interior, coming up with the keys that dangled from the ignition.

What was he doing? Jack had told him to hide. He could be over the ridge and down in those rocks by now. Instead, he was searching the rear seat and retrieving the shotgun he spotted there. Why hadn't he forced Meadow to come with him?

Meadow opened the door. She had found some clothing, beige jeans rolled at the ankle and an oversize T-shirt both of which only made her look smaller and more vulnerable.

"Well, here are my guardian angels. Did my father send you?"

"Yes, Ms. Wrangler. If you'll come with us."

He couldn't see her but he heard her sandals crunch on the gravel on the other side of the vehicle.

"Where is Mr. Tehauno?"

"Oh, he's down below looking for his friend, William Cheney. I told him he was gone."

Dylan tried to figure how her father's people knew that he and Meadow were together. He'd made one transmission. All other communication had gone only to Jack Bear Den, whom he trusted with his life. That meant someone had monitored the shortwave communication and sent these men.

Dylan checked the shotgun and found two rounds. He flipped the lever to single shot.

"We have orders to collect him, as well," said the second man.

Yeah. That is not happening, Dylan thought.

The sun was behind them now, making its ascent on one of the longest days of the year. Sweat beaded on Dylan's skin as he waited in the blistering hot morning sun. He bet it would be over a hundred today, too. The question was whether either he or Meadow would live to see it.

Dylan reached the back bumper of the Humvee and glanced in the rear window, spotting an empty back compartment.

"Well, I'd like to get out of here, so you'll have to come back for him."

"Have a look inside," said the commander.

"He's not there, I said."

"After that, check the perimeter." He glanced at his smartphone. "He's close."

The driver pushed past Meadow, who managed to look indignant rather than frightened. She had to know that she'd made the wrong call remaining behind, but she held on to her persona as the powerful daughter of a powerful man.

The redhead disappeared into the gatehouse and returned a few moments later. "Not there."

"There's no cover but the rocks. Check the hill on the west." Then he turned to Meadow. "Right this way, Ms. Wrangler."

But, instead of going meekly along, Meadow screamed a warning.

"Dylan! Run!"

Her abductor dropped all pretext and slapped her across the face. Meadow staggered but remained standing. A few minutes later Dylan heard the crunch of boots on gravel as the second man returned.

"I didn't see him."

The one holding Meadow cursed.

"Get in the car," he said, presumably to Meadow.

"I'm not going anywhere with you. And when my father finds out that you struck me, you'll be sitting in a jail cell, mister." There was a scuffle and then Meadow's voice again. "Hey! Let go of me."

They were heading his way. Dylan raised the shotgun and took one breath in preparation. Then he stood, revealing his position.

The young driver did not look up as he muscled Meadow along and, behind her, the veteran soldier held a Taser pointed at Meadow's back. He spotted Dylan, his step slowing as they made eye contact.

"Don't!" said Dylan, but it was too late.

The older man pressed the trigger at the same moment his gaze flicked to Dylan. Meadow jerked and twitched, falling to her knees and then out of Dylan's line of sight.

Red, the young one, reached for his sidearm, still locked in the holster by a black nylon strap.

Dylan swung the shotgun at him, aiming at his face.

"It's the last thing you'll do," he said.

Red lifted his hands. Dylan swung the weapon to

the real threat, who continued to press the Taser trigger. Dylan's heart hammered as he realized he was trying to kill Meadow by giving her enough juice to stop her heart.

"Drop it!" he commanded, and raised the stock of his rifle to his cheek, aiming for center mass.

The older one dropped the Taser.

Meadow went still. Was she even breathing?

Chapter Ten

Dylan held his aim on the one in charge as he spoke to the younger man.

"Put her in the Humvee," said Dylan.

Dylan had an adequate view of the ginger-headed man from his periphery. The man glanced at his supervisor, who gave a slight inclination of his head. Meadow was lifted, slack and limp, into the rear seat of the Humvee.

"Now step away," said Dylan.

If he had any doubt about Meadow's innocence in this, this attack had banished it. She was a victim here. At worst, she was a pawn.

"You going to kill us, son?" asked the older one.

"No, I don't think so. You're the golden boy. Clean service record. Always making the right moves, even on the basketball court. Always following orders." He took a step closer. "Thing is, in all that time in the service, you never did have to shoot anyone. Look them in the eye and take their life. Because that would be wrong. And you don't do wrong."

"Stop," Dylan ordered.

"You aren't a killer. Give me the gun, son." He extended his hand and Dylan knew the man had badly underestimated him. Just because he *had* not did not mean he *would* not. He would—to protect Meadow, he knew he would do anything.

"I promised to protect her."

"She's not worth your time, son. Black eye to the whole family. Never held a job and she's got more men than a stray dog got fleas. You'd be the flavor of the month. And that's just not you."

Another step and his target would be close enough to take the shotgun barrel. Dylan knew a shot at this range would take his life and he knew the scatter pattern of shot from the years shooting on the rez. So, when he pulled the trigger, he aimed low and wide. The outside edge of the shot scatter struck his opponent in the leg and he went down howling like a wolf.

Dylan ordered the other man to lie face down beside his commander. Then he checked Meadow and found a pulse. He couldn't control the need to see her safe anymore than he could leave her here to die.

Flavor of the month? Maybe, but at least he'd be walking out of here.

The younger one was crying. Dylan took his pistol, phone and sunglasses.

"Pass code," said Dylan.

The crying man gave it to him. Dylan used the phone to call Jack but got flipped over to voice mail. That meant Jack was out of range. Dylan held the phone out, wondering how long the recording lasted.

"Your name," said Dylan.

"Vic Heil."

"Why are you two here?"

"Retrieve Meadow Wrangler."

"Who are you working for?"

"Wrangler. That's all I know. I swear."

The injured man howled and cursed at Vic. The only intelligible words were "Shut up."

"Did you two set the blast that started the fire?"

No answer.

Dylan pressed the pistol to Heil's temple.

"Did you?"

"Yes!"

"Why?"

"I don't know. Take out the snitch. That's what the captain said."

"What snitch?"

"Shut up," shrieked his commander. Dylan stepped on his bleeding thigh, and the man howled again.

"Williams," said Heil. "He's a snitch. Blabbing to someone. That's all I know. I swear."

"Blabbing to whom?"

"Don't know, I said."

"You don't know or they don't know?"

"I don't know."

Dylan removed the barrel from the man's head.

"Shut up!" yelled the captain, clutching his leg and rolling side to side on his back.

"Come on, man," said Heil to Dylan. "He's bleeding all over the place."

"Why do you want the girl?" asked Dylan.

"Just find her, is all."

Dylan lifted the phone and checked. The call had disconnected. He found the microphone app and pressed Record.

"What's the captain's name?"

"Rubins."

"First name?"

"Don't know."

Captain Rubins rolled from side to side as his leg oozed blood from the many punctures.

"Say it again," Dylan ordered. He held out the phone.

Vic started talking, telling what he knew, which wasn't much with the captain yelling at him that they'd just signed their own death warrants. Vic did admit to setting the fire and told him where they'd set the charges. He said he didn't know who they worked for and Dylan believed him. When he ordered him up, Vic pissed himself, but Dylan still sent him walking down the ridge. Dylan knew that Vic expected the second shotgun blast to hit him in the back. Dylan just wanted him far enough away to give him time to get Meadow out of here.

He turned to Rubins.

"You want to fill in the blanks?"

"Yeah," he said through gritted teeth, "you're a dead man. They won't stop."

"Why does her father want her dead?" asked Dylan.

The man's smile was a snarl. "Run, Bobcat. The BEARs are coming."

They knew he was called Bobcat. What else did they know?

Dylan took the man's phone and the pistol strapped to his bleeding thigh.

"I'll send help," he said as he climbed into the Humvee.

Rubins snarled. "You'll need it more than me."

Dylan commandeered their vehicle.

He needed to find the Turquoise Canyon Hotshots. Jack had given him their position, but he had doubts he could reach them on the main road. The Hummer gave him some leeway on the route. If there was any area of back burn, he might get Meadow through. But where to then? He didn't know. He only knew that they couldn't stay here.

They wound down the road that led toward the line of smoke billowing skyward. How many acres had already burned?

Halfway around they saw Heil still walking in wet pants. He watched them drive past and then reversed course. Dylan used the Humvee's satellite link to call 911 and report the injured man. He said the man had been injured by the discharge of a shotgun and gave the location. He had a feeling that Rubins was too stubborn to die. If Heil slowed the bleeding and the shot pellets had missed the femoral artery, Rubins would likely survive.

Dylan pulled to a stop to check Meadow. Other than the two marks on her back from the Taser, she seemed fine. Her heartbeat was normal and so was her breathing. He used some of the water in the Humvee to wet her face. Her eyes fluttered open and she groaned.

"What happened?"

He told her.

She rubbed her jaw. "Feels like someone punched me." Her hand moved to her head. "Worst hangover ever."

"Drink some water." He offered the bottle to her and she drank.

"They Tasered me?" she asked.

"In the back."

She rubbed her forehead. "I should have listened to you. I'm sorry, Dylan."

"They hit you when you tried to warn me."

She glanced away.

"That was dangerous," he said.

"Yeah, well, reckless is what I'm good at. Remember?"

"That wasn't reckless. It was selfless."

Her artifice dropped with her smile and she gave him a serious look. "I didn't want anything to happen to you."

Now he was the one who had lost his mask. He didn't know what to say. He had never expected this woman—this woman he thought to be a spoiled little rich girl—to show such courage. Just like everyone else, he'd underestimated her.

"How'd you get us away?"

He gave her the short version.

"What were they going to do with me?"

"Nothing good. Those guys set the fire."

She groaned. "Help me to the front seat."

He lifted her easily, then settled her into the passenger seat and buckled her in.

"How do you know they set it?"

Dylan wondered if he should tell her about the recording he had gotten. After a mental debate, he revealed he had Heil's confession.

"It implicates my father," she said.

He nodded.

She glanced away. "I can't believe this. I thought…
I believed he loved me."

"Maybe he loves the cause more."

She said nothing to that.

Dylan called home and got his grandpa again after
seven rings. His grandpa wasn't fast. But he was a
wonderful fisherman and had also turned his turquoise claim over to Dylan. His older sisters Rita and
Gianna didn't want it, but did want occasional nodules
of the bright blue stone.

"Where are we going?" asked Meadow.

He told her his plan to find a break in the fire line,
one as close to his home team of hotshots as possible.

She glanced ahead. "The fire line again?"

"We have to get through it. The crews will be on
site. They'll have a break somewhere." He hoped.

There was only one road, so he followed it as far
as he could. She turned to look at the place where the
hull of her car sat. The ground was scorched now,
black and stinking of smoke. He drove toward the fire,
hoping he would get a signal but knowing the smoke
would interfere with reception.

Dylan got them as far as the ridge of smoke, looking for a break or a crew at work. The last thing he
wanted was to get himself into another spot where
they would be trapped. He couldn't tell if the smoke
was worse or if it was only because the winds had
shifted. It grew so thick he needed the headlights to
keep going. Meadow pointed to the sky.

"Look!"

He glanced up at the helicopter flying with the red
collapsible bucket beneath. A moment later it released

the load and red fire suppressant spilled from the sky. The compound was sticky and slimy, but it worked. He headed for the spot the chopper had dropped the payload. A few minutes later he saw the place where the ground was coated with the viscous red fluid. Then he saw the men behind it making a line.

The phone Dylan had taken from Rubins rang and he lifted it, not recognizing the number. He picked up.

"Yeah," he said.

"You got them?"

"Yeah."

"Where the hell are you?"

"Heading for the fire line."

"Fire line? You're supposed to call for a chopper."

"Send it."

"Who the hell is this?" There was cursing. Then the line went dead.

"Well, that didn't work."

"You don't speak like them."

"I was trying."

"Your speech pattern is more lilting, like a song."

Dylan didn't know if he liked that.

"Can we get through the fire line?" she asked.

"Jack says so. He also says the main road is open, but it will be covered with highway patrol. We don't want that."

"Won't they help us?"

He came from a place where the police were not often helpful. He supposed her parents had told her to look for a policeman if she were in trouble.

"You and I are wanted for starting this fire," he reminded her.

"But we didn't do it."

He thought that was irrelevant.

"We just have to explain."

"Meadow, a man was killed up here. Your father sent killers to finish you. He won't help you and, without your father's money, you will be represented by an attorney appointed by the court. You could be in jail a very long time while they investigate the case—that is, if someone doesn't get to you while you are locked up. Do you have anything to prove your innocence?"

"You can't prove you didn't do something."

"Exactly."

"I was with you."

"You were in position to film the explosion. You had an opportunity to set the charges. I did, too. Plus, if those men are to be believed, your father not only set you up to die in this fire, he sent men to be certain you didn't reappear with a different story. He might try again."

"I could go to my sisters or brothers."

He didn't know them and so didn't trust them.

"If you like."

"They might be with him." She sank into her seat. "I have no one. That's what you're saying."

"You have me."

"All right, Bobcat. What do we do?"

"Find out who set the fire. Clear our names. Bring the guilty to justice."

"And how do we do all that?"

"Working on it."

Chapter Eleven

"I've never seen anything like it," Meadow said as she glanced out the window.

Dylan had. Many times in many states, he realized as he left the main road to weave through the charred remains of standing trees. The odor of smoke seeped in through the vents.

"Hard to believe now, but the vegetation will come back."

"Ruined the view from the valley. I suppose that was the point."

That seemed very likely. Dylan followed the helicopters, judging where they had been and choosing his route from that. When they reached the area that had received a coating of the red fire retardant slurry, the first crew he met was out of Flagstaff. They directed him to the Apache crew, but that turned out to be the Navajo boys out of Fort Defiance. They knew where the Turquoise Canyon crew was working and Dylan found them, making a line with their axes, their motions smooth and efficient. He paused a moment to see how well they were managing without their former crew chief.

Ray Strong left the line to speak to him. His face was streaked with sweat and soot, making his teeth appear especially bright. Even without trying, there was a kind of perpetual devilment in his twinkling eyes and mischievous smile. Ray had been in and out of trouble most of his life, owing to a reckless nature coupled with a stubborn streak. But he was one man Dylan knew he could rely on. In his current situation, he needed a friend who didn't care very much for rules or laws.

Dylan left the vehicle to greet his friend, with Meadow close behind him.

Ray hugged him, and Dylan accepted a thump on the back.

"We've been looking for you all night," said Ray. "News reported you both dead. I see Jack was right, again. Man, you gave me a scare." Ray broke away and gave Meadow a long look. Dylan tried to tamp down his possessiveness as Ray moved closer, and failed. He objected to the way Ray smiled at her and gripped her hand during the introduction. He held on a little too long, in Dylan's opinion.

"How's Morgan?" asked Dylan.

Ray was now a married man with an instant family, since Morgan had a daughter from a previous relationship.

Ray seemed to be holding back a laugh as he regarded Dylan. "Just fine. Worried about you, too. Let's get you two back to base. It's not too far."

Ray rode with them. The base was just a grouping of tents, a temporary shower area and a food drop. Ray left them to return to the line, as Dylan and Meadow shared a ready-made meal. They were still eating when Ray reappeared.

"Highway boys are here. They're looking for you two. They already have your Humvee."

Dylan was on his feet looking for an escape route. He needed a vehicle.

"Your truck here?"

Ray shook his head. "Came in by bus."

They were trapped.

"Hide in plain sight," said Ray, holding up two fire helmets.

Dylan wrapped Meadow's blue hair in a bandana then adjusted a helmet to fit her head. In short order, Dylan was dressed in familiar attire, borrowed from Ray, and Ray had a quick version of all that had happened since Dylan and Meadow had been forced into the fire shelter. Well, not everything. He'd left out what had happened in the shower and what had been happening to him since. If they survived this, he'd like to take her out.

The voice of reason scoffed. Where? Where in the wild world would an Apache hotshot take a celebrity heiress? The impossibility of a relationship weighed on him as much as the fear of pursuit.

"We need to get you into protection. Like Carter. Until then, you two hide on the line."

Meadow slipped into a pair of battered boots that Ray offered. She could keep them on if she laced them tight.

"Jack said Forrest is here somewhere. The feds are out here looking for you, too. We need to be sure that Jack finds you first."

"Our crew chief is right up here," said one of his men, a little too loudly as he came up the hill in their direction. "Captain?" he hollered. "There are two detectives from the Highway Patrol wanting to see you."

Ray waved Dylan and Meadow away and they retreated in the opposite direction.

"Mr. Strong, we need the location of the two fugitives that arrived in a Hummer."

Dylan heard Ray speaking to one officer.

"Where's the other one?" he whispered to Meadow.

"What?"

"Ray's man said there were two. Where's the other one?"

The male voice came from behind him. "Right here."

Dylan had a weapon. Two, actually, but he would not draw on a law enforcement officer. He raised his hands. Meadow did the same.

"Facedown on the ground. Both of you."

Dylan stretched out. Meadow hesitated.

"Meadow, do as he says," said Dylan.

The officer took out his Taser and Meadow dropped down beside Dylan. In a moment they had their hands zip-tied behind their back, they were frisked, read their rights and were then hustled into the back of an Arizona Highway Patrol vehicle.

He saw Ray make an attempt to get to them. They were both members of Tribal Thunder, and he knew Ray would do whatever it took to get him out.

Ray called out to Dylan in Tonto Apache.

"I will call help. Do not worry, Brother Bobcat."

Dylan replied in Tonto, "Hurry, my brother. Her father wants her dead."

The last he saw of Ray was his worried face as he drew out his radio. Then they were gone, driving past the staging area and away from the fire.

"Where are we going?" asked Dylan.

"Flagstaff."

"I want a lawyer," said Meadow. Then she turned to him and said, "Don't you say a thing to any of them until I get you an attorney."

She still didn't understand. All her money and power and influence flowed from her parents and that tap had been shut off. Meadow now had only her reputation and her fame. It wouldn't be enough.

They were met en route by the Flagstaff police and escorted to the station. Once there, they were greeted by news crews with cameras and microphones pointed at them like artillery.

For the first time in his life, Dylan found himself on the wrong end of the law. He had always done what was expected, what was right and legal. He'd helped Ray Strong out of more situations and scrapes than he could count, but Dylan had never been the one facing a prison cell.

They were separated for processing. Dylan's one call at six that evening was to his grandfather, who said he would send help. Dylan asked him to get to their shaman, Kenshaw Little Falcon. He then spent much of the next day refusing to answer questions. The police did furnish him with some information. The vehicle they had taken was found to have carried explosives. Some of the blasting cord was still in the

back. They told him that they believed he was one of
the eco-extremists involved with the theft down at
the Lilac Copper Mine. They were testing the explosives and expected a match. He did not confirm or
deny his ownership of the Humvee, but it didn't matter, because the registration bore his name. Clearly, he
and Meadow had more than just terrible timing. They
were the fall guys for this and were supposed to die
like good little patsies. He expected someone would
be sent to get to them. That was what had been done
to the Lilac mine shooter. The hit had been made as
the mass gunman was transported to the police station in Darabee. Sanchez had been assassinated by
one of Dylan's own people, and whatever Sanchez
had known died with him.

The police needed the guilty and BEAR needed a
scapegoat. Dylan thought they had found two. And
the fact that he had been driving the vehicle and that
Meadow's brother headed PAN, the organization
known in the Southwest for Protecting All Nature,
and that her father was an environmental documentary
filmmaker did not help her cause. She came across
as some Patty Hearst–like character. The rich-girl-
turned-terrorist. Oh, boy, would that sell papers.

Dylan wondered how long they would keep at this.
It seemed like hours since he'd arrived, but in the
windowless interrogation room it was difficult to tell.

The interrogating officer started asking him the
same questions again from the beginning. Dylan exhaled his frustration and kept his mouth firmly shut.

The impact from something heavy shook the building. The detectives stood and looked at the door.

"What was that?" asked the younger detective.

"See what's up," said the one with the sprinkling of gray in his short stubble of hair.

"Felt like a bomb." The man already had the door open when they heard the sound of automatic weapon fire. The older man shot out the door and then turned back to the junior man and aimed a finger at Dylan.

"Watch him!" Then he vanished from sight.

The younger detective watched him go and so did not see Dylan rise from his seat and charge him. The impact of that attack brought them both out into the hallway, where Dylan landed on top of him. He stood preparing to stomp the guy if he needed to, but the officer had the wind knocked out of him, giving Dylan the moment he needed to retrieve the man's wallet and the handcuff key. That was where his friend Jack Bear Den kept his key. Dylan also took the guy's car keys. If the fob was right, the guy drove a Dodge. Dylan had one wrist out of the cuffs when the detective reached for his gun. Dylan hit him in the jaw and then dragged him back into the interrogation room. Then Bobcat went hunting for Meadow.

Where was she? He didn't know what was happening, but he knew who they were after—him and Meadow, the loose ends that could ruin their plans.

The police returned fire now. Automatic weapon blasts mingled with the discharge of shotguns. Dylan checked one room after another. He found her in an interrogation room with a wide-eyed female officer. Dylan ordered her back and she went for her weapon. Meadow was up and diving for the female officer, causing her to fall to the ground and her pistol to skitter across the floor.

Dylan dragged Meadow off and hustled her out. Her hands were cuffed, but he didn't stop to address her captured wrists.

"What's happening?" she asked.

"Don't know." He turned away from the gunfire and made it to the end of the hall that led to an emergency exit and then stairs. The Flagstaff joint police and sheriff building had only two floors. They were halfway down the flight when they heard the door above them open. Dylan glanced up as they made the turn around the landing and saw Vic Heil, one of the two men who had crashed the gatehouse.

"They're here," Vic yelled over his shoulder.

Then Vic aimed the automatic weapon at them. Dylan pushed Meadow to the wall as the blast of gunfire hit the concrete stairs above their heads.

"Who is it?" she asked.

"Guy from the gatehouse. Run, Meadow."

They burst out the side door, triggering another alarm. Dylan blinked at the bright sunlight and the blast of hot air.

Meadow stumbled, her hands still cuffed behind her back. Dylan kept a hand on her elbow to assist her balance as they darted into the parking lot. Meadow was quick and they made it out the door to the rear parking area. They darted between the closest cars and kept low as Dylan retrieved the fob and pressed the door release. They heard a beep and headed for the sound as the back door of the building banged open. Their pursuer had reached the parking lot.

Chapter Twelve

Dylan did not hit the lock release again for fear of alerting the gunman of their destination. Instead, he searched for Dodge vehicles. His second try found a car that was unlocked. He got Meadow into the passenger seat and then ducked around to the driver's side, praying that this was the detective's vehicle and not just an unlocked car.

The key turned and the motor engaged. His relief was short-lived as he saw the gunman's head turn in their direction. An instant later, the gunman was running. Dylan saw him clearly now, the younger man from the gatehouse—Vic Heil. Behind him came a second man that Dylan did not know.

Dylan threw the muscle car into Reverse and flew backward in the Dodge Challenger. Thank goodness the detective liked fast cars. This one was a V-8.

Dylan burned rubber and fishtailed on his exit from the lot. Meadow looked back, yelped and ducked low as bullets peppered the trunk.

Vic had missed the tires, Dylan realized as he made the main road and screeched out into traffic amid the sound of horn blasts. They barreled away from the station. Dylan didn't know where he was headed yet. He just wanted to put distance between him and the men who hunted them.

"Hit men," said Meadow. "Honest-to-God hit men." She let her head sink back to the seat and turned to look at him. "You saved my life again."

"You're welcome," he said, and cast her a grin. He drove them out of the city before stopping to release the second side of his cuffs and set Meadow free.

"Where should we go?"

"Two choices. Your family or mine," he said.

"My family has financial resources."

"They also might have sent those men to kill us."

"I've always wanted to see those reservoirs in the mountains," she said. "And the ridge of turquoise you spoke about."

With the destination decided, Dylan set them in motion. Twilight found them driving south. It was well past dark when they reached Indian land. Dylan thought it was the first time he had taken an easy breath in two days.

Dylan drove straight down I-17, the fastest way home from Flagstaff. He stopped to make a phone call at a truck stop east of Phoenix and reached Jack. His friend met them at the boundary of their land. He flashed his lights and escorted them toward tribal headquarters. Their tribe was small—only a little over 900 members living on the rez—so the tribal seat included a small police station in a wing of the building, but it was enough for the nine officers on the payroll.

Dylan needed a shower, a hot meal and a warm bed. The thought of bed made his gaze slide to Meadow.

"How are you holding up?" he asked.

"Exhausted. Do you think he'll interrogate us again?"

"He'll have questions, but I'll handle them."

She levered her palm under her chin as if she needed to brace herself to keep her head up. Her yawn triggered one of his own.

He pulled into tribal headquarters behind Jack. His friend Detective Jack Bear Den stepped from his vehicle. Meadow's gasp at the sight of him was audible.

"He's…he's…" She was pointing now, leaning forward.

"I know. He's big."

"Big? That's a giant. He's Apache?"

"There's some debate about that," he muttered.

She turned to him, her voice conspiratorial. "Really?"

Dylan must be more exhausted than he realized, revealing Jack's business.

"He has brothers, but he doesn't really resemble them."

She nodded, those pretty brown eyes wide. "Gotcha."

Jack was at her door now, drawing it open.

"Miss Wrangler?"

She nodded.

"Welcome to Turquoise Canyon. I'm tribal police detective Jack Bear Den. I'm sorry to hear of your troubles."

He extended a hand. Dylan could not explain why

it pleased him that she looked to him before accepting. He nodded and she took Jack's hand, her small one all but disappearing into his.

"Thank you," Meadow said.

Dylan got out of the car to join them as they made their way into the station.

"I ordered some food," said Jack. "Should be waiting."

Dylan wanted a shower, but he thanked his friend. Jack was a fellow member of Tribal Thunder and a warrior by nature. It was because of Jack that his brother Carter had survived the insurgent attack that had killed their translator and their friend Hatch Yeager. Carter had rescued their sergeant, and Jack had passed the wounded man to Dylan, then grabbed a hold of Carter to keep him from charging into the enemy forces that had already overtaken Hatch's position. It was exactly the kind of cool thinking under pressure that made Dylan so relieved to have reached the tribe and Jack's protection.

Jack escorted Meadow into the station and then introduced her to his police chief, Wallace Tinnin. Once in the staff room, Dylan was greeted by three members of the tribal council. As was custom, they spoke of generalities until their guest was fed. Only after their meal did they speak of what had happened, and they chose to speak in Tonto Apache.

The short version was that they believed Dylan was innocent of all charges and were prepared to protect him from any and all Anglos. Meadow was a different story, however. They looked at her with suspicion and feared that this outsider would bring trouble. It was only through Dylan's refusal to desert her that she was permitted to stay.

Dylan made the decision to take her to his home. Jack arranged police protection for them. Dylan knew resources were tight and appreciated Tinnin approving the decision.

His home was in a remote area, past the tribal community of Koun'nde. Access was via a single road. One way in. One way out. Jack escorted him home and Dylan was relieved to see his place was empty. He'd been half-afraid that his mother, sisters and grandfather might be there to greet him. He loved his family, but his energy was waning. He needed rest.

Jack went in first while Dylan and Meadow waited outside.

"He's like a pit bull," said Meadow.

"Just bull. No pit."

"He's in your warrior society?" she asked.

Dylan nodded and stretched his tight muscles.

"What's his spirit animal? Wait, let me guess. Buffalo."

Dylan shook his head, his smile turning sad. He rubbed the back of his neck.

"Bear?" she guessed.

"No. Our shaman, Kenshaw Little Falcon, did not choose an animal for Jack. Jack was given the medicine wheel."

Her brow wrinkled. "That's what?"

"It looks like a compass, divided into the four directions. But the symbol is more inclusive, with many meanings."

"Why did he choose that?"

"I do not know. I only know what Jack told us, that Kenshaw said it would help him find which direction to go."

Dylan was about to tell her that there was one more difference between Jack and the three other newest members of Tribal Thunder. Jack's tattoo was not on his right arm, but emblazoned on his back, between his shoulder blades. But somehow that seemed even more private than the mystery of his birth, so he remained silent.

Jack's return ended Dylan's internal quandary.

"All clear," said Jack. "See you in the morning. Kenshaw wants to speak to you tomorrow."

Dylan stiffened. He had never had any trouble with their shaman until February, when Jack had mentioned his suspicions that Kenshaw was an active member of WOLF.

WOLF, which stood for Wilderness of Life Forever, was the less extreme of the two groups. Their aim was the same as BEAR, but they made all efforts to preserve human life while BEAR made efforts to destroy as many lives as possible in their efforts to protect and preserve nature.

If their shaman was an eco-extremist, seeing him might put Meadow in danger.

Dylan switched to Apache. "Do you still suspect he is a member of WOLF?"

"No. I no longer suspect. I know he is."

Dylan lifted a brow.

"I will not put her in danger."

Now Jack lifted a brow, and Dylan found it hard to hold his gaze.

"Really? Do you know what you are doing?"

"I used to think so."

"You saved her, so she is your responsibility. But be careful. Even I have heard of this one." He inclined his head toward Meadow, who seemed to know she was the subject of conversation as she looked from one to the other.

"I am always careful," said Dylan.

Jack smiled. Did he think he was speaking to Ray? One or the other of them was always reminding Ray to be careful. To follow the rules. To do as he was told. No one had ever felt the need to issue such advice to Dylan. Suddenly he understood the sour look he always gleaned when he gave his unsolicited advice to Ray. He glared at Jack and switched to English.

"We will see you in the morning."

"I'll call first." He let that one sink in and then tipped his cowboy hat to Meadow. "Sleep well, Ms. Wrangler."

They watched him walk away.

"He doesn't like me," said Meadow.

Dylan didn't deny it. But what mattered was that Dylan liked her. She wasn't what she believed herself to be. He recalled her tackling the female officer in Flagstaff and running through the parking lot. Meadow was a warrior and a survivor, just like Dylan. But there were so many differences between them. Too many, he reminded himself. Still, reason didn't stop him from admiring her, and, if he was honest, he'd admit his feelings did not end with a growing respect. He was beginning to like her. And for the first time since he had met her, they were safe and alone together.

Chapter Thirteen

Meadow explored his living room, feeling his gaze follow her as she moved through Dylan's space. The furniture was sparse, nearly Spartan with the exception of a long, sagging couch and an upholstered chair and ottoman. The back of the sofa was draped with a woolen blanket in a bold geometric pattern that reminded her of a Navajo rug. Behind the chair sat a floor lamp angled to pour light on the occupant. On the ottoman were three stacks of books and on the floor, in the place where an end table might be, sat another pile of books reaching up to the level of the armrest. She saw mysteries, thrillers, books about American history and a travel guide on fishing in Alaska. Dylan had more books on his ottoman than she'd read in the past six years. She hadn't read anything much since her schooling ended and she no longer had to state the theme of the fish in *The Old Man and the Sea* or describe the meaning of irony using Lord Byron's *Don Juan*. She looked to the place where a television would be and found only a speaker system that attached to an MP3 player and a charging station for digital devices.

"You don't watch TV?" she asked.

"On my tablet, sometimes. I like college hoops."

"News?"

"Online mostly. Can I get you a drink?"

"Wine would be wonderful. Red, if you have it."

He glanced away. "I don't. Never drank alcohol."

She did not succeed in stifling a gasp. "Never?"

Now she wondered if he had a problem, but he'd said he never drank, not that he didn't drink or didn't drink anymore. She had given up hard liquor while in detox, after a late-night swim lead to an indecency charge. She now only drank wine and held herself to a two-glass limit.

"Because you're Native American?"

He smiled. "Because alcohol is bad for you and makes you do things you later regret."

"That's true."

"No one in my family drinks."

"Is everyone in your family Apache?"

"Yes, all."

"And you only date other Apache?"

"That's a small gene pool. I don't limit myself or discriminate by race. Though my mom would prefer..." He glanced away and made a face.

He didn't have to finish. His mother wanted a nice Native American girl. She certainly didn't want a spoiled white girl with Smurf-blue hair whose main talent seemed to be generating income for the tabloids.

"Maybe I can meet her sometime." She felt singularly inadequate. Generally, she only felt this way when with her siblings. Her wealth often put men off balance, but lately her lifestyle had attracted men who liked money and especially liked spending hers.

"Oh, I'm sure you will. The minute she finds out I'm home, she'll be at the door."

Meadow looked at the door in question and swallowed hard. She glanced down at her clothing and grimaced. She thought she could still smell the odor of smoke clinging to her.

"I can't meet her like this," she said.

Dylan smiled. "I think you are safe for the night."

She didn't want to be safe. And she wanted more than a night. More than a few days, a lost weekend. Oh, she was in so much trouble. He was a warrior, a hotshot, a man of character with morals strongly rooted in his community. She was a punch line.

"So, tomorrow we speak to your shaman?"

"That's right."

"Is there any protocol or anything?"

"It's not like meeting the Queen of England. You don't have to curtsy. He's a regular guy, mostly."

"So women can speak to him?"

He smiled. "Again, not Hassidic. Not Amish. Apache."

She flushed. "I don't know anything about shamans."

"They learn by apprenticeship. It's a calling, like priests, but they are not celibate. They preside over ceremonies like the Sunrise Ceremony, which is a woman's coming of age. He advises, prays, heals, and is a spiritual leader. He preserves our language and culture by teaching the youth."

Somehow she could see Dylan doing all those things.

"Are you considering it?"

He inhaled. "How did you know that?"

"Just the way you looked when you spoke of their responsibilities."

"I've considered it. I'm a little old to begin."

"Have you spoken to your shaman?"

"Yes, and he's agreed to accept me as an apprentice."

"But you can still marry?" As soon as she said it, she recognized her mistake. Was it the haste of her words or the worry in her eyes that told him her thoughts? She didn't know, but she saw the confusion break into speculation as he considered why she asked this question.

When she realized she was wringing her hands, she dropped them to her sides. Now she felt small and inadequate again.

"What?" she asked.

"You're a puzzle," he said. "You could have any man. I'm struggling to understand your interest in me. Is it just physical?"

Something told her to withdraw, protect her ego. If she said yes, he might sleep with her, but he might also tell her that he was not that kind of guy. But to admit that she wanted more than to share his bed was to show a kind of need and vulnerability that frightened her nearly as much as the fire shelter. She looked at him.

He waited, his dark eyes cautious. Was that the glimmer of hope?

She bit her bottom lip and then jumped in head-first, like always.

"It's not just physical. I'm attracted to you, physically, of course. Powerfully, and since I first saw you."

"You were rude when you first saw me."

"I was showing off. Trying to get your attention."

"You succeeded."

"I acted like an ass."

"But back to your attraction," he said, stepping closer.

"I've never met anyone like you," she said.

"Apache?"

"Yes, but no. You're protective, perceptive, sensitive."

"Sensitive? I'll deny that if you tell anyone."

"You shouldn't. It's rare."

He took her hand and led her down the hall. "Let's finish the tour."

"Kitchen is through there."

She had a glimpse of a dark room with empty counters.

"I have two bedrooms and one bath. The tribe provides housing through HUD. We own the land and property on the land communally. Unlike most tribes, we do not have a shortage of housing and so a single man like me can live in a single home."

"That's good."

"We have a surplus because of a falling birthrate and because unemployment has caused many of our young men to leave us to find work elsewhere."

"Like Alaska?"

His eyebrows lifted again and then he glanced back to the living room. "You got that from the book on salmon fishing?"

"And knowing that there are jobs there."

"There are. But I would not like to leave the tribe for so long. I see what happens. Men leave. They find work or a woman and…" He shrugged. "Men go to the woman's family. It's tradition here and common out there, too."

Like his brothers. They had both left and never come back.

"You speak as if it's another country. We live in the same state."

"But a different world. I don't know if I could blend my life with an Anglo."

She let her hand slip away.

"But maybe the right woman could change that," he said.

The hope bubbled in her chest like a tiny gem. The oyster making a pearl of possibilities inside her hard shell. Was she the right woman?

Her skin was tingling and she felt the flush of excitement.

"You are a fascinating woman. Brazen. Independent and very brave."

"I never was brave."

"Maybe you never had anything worth fighting for before."

There was truth in that.

He motioned to a door. "Guest room."

She glanced in and saw a full-size bed made up with military precision with a striped red, black and turquoise wool blanket and white sheets. There was a desk with a computer.

"Office?"

"Something like it. My room is across the hall. Bathroom is between the two. We each have a door lock. You can use it if you don't want company."

His smile faded as his joke turned into possibilities. Was he also remembering the shower they had shared? Did he regret setting her aside? She took a step toward him, vowing that if she ever got him naked again, she wasn't going to let him go.

"Need anything else?" he asked, and then pressed his lips together as he realized what he had offered.

"Yes," she said, and looped her arms around his neck. The kiss she gave him was full of sensual need and promise. He responded instantly, gathering her tight in his arms so she could feel every muscular curve and contour and hard ridge.

She hummed with satisfaction as he deepened the kiss, bending her over his arm. Her fingers raked his back, calling on his spirit animal to take his mate. The sound he made was a growl, deep, low and dangerous. Oh, she wanted to unleash that danger. Meadow raked her fingers downward.

He gasped and then pushed her back. She felt the past repeating and wondered if she'd ever recover from the humiliation of throwing herself at him twice.

But this time he didn't reject her. The heat in his gaze made her stomach tremble.

"Are you sure, Meadow?" he asked.

She shivered with desire fused with anticipation. In answer she used one index finger to graze down him midline, stopping at his waistband, where she hooked that finger inside the fabric of his trousers and tugged.

"Very," she said, just before his mouth claimed hers again.

She savored the sweet velvet glide of his tongue on hers. Dylan's hand angled up under the shirt and unfastened the oversize jeans she wore. She broke the kiss to kick out of her borrowed boots and stepped clear of the men's pants, returning to him and their kiss.

The pads of his fingers grazed over her thigh, making her stomach tremble. She wanted him to touch her there at the epicenter of the pulsing need he stirred.

Meadow rubbed against the hard muscle of his thigh and was rewarded when he splayed his fingers over her bottom and lifted her until their hips met. She wrapped her legs about him, locking her ankles behind his back as he turned them toward the bed.

He was whispering to her in his language, his breath stirring the hairs on her neck. The anticipation beat inside her like a living thing, the need pulsing with her blood.

"Hurry," she said.

"No. This is not going to be fast. When you look back on your life, Meadow, I want you to remember me."

Was he already planning their separation? Perhaps he was just wise enough to see the number of obstacles between them. A realist, when she had always been a dreamer.

And her dreams were full of Dylan, now and forever. Oh, she would remember him. How could she ever forget? She only hoped that she would look back and remember this as the beginning and not the end.

What would convince him to stay, to give them a chance? Certainly nothing in the bed that even now rushed up to greet her. She needed to touch more than his body.

But his body was what she needed right now— the warmth and comfort and protection. He'd never denied her those things, and she knew that he would deny her nothing tonight.

Chapter Fourteen

Dylan explored Meadow's body with both hands. She wanted him, and tonight it did not matter that there was no future in it. His time in the service had taught him the tenuousness of life. Since his return, he'd forgotten this lesson. But the wildfire had made him remember that life was sweet and short and never to be taken for granted.

They were safe and she was in his arms. What more could he wish for? A future with her. Well, yes, but he'd whisper that only to himself, the irrational desire that told him this woman was placed on this earth only to walk at his side.

He longed to give her so much more than his protection. He wanted to give her his heart. And that would be foolish, indeed. She'd made it clear she was not the sort of woman to be trusted with something as fragile as a man's love. She was giving him this night and he would take what he could, knowing that his family would not approve of her or of his actions. Knowing that his medicine society would be shocked to see the golden boy make such an obvious mistake.

He let the pads of his fingers graze over the soft,

yielding flesh, stroking down her midline, pausing at her navel and feeling her stomach muscles ripple under his touch. He followed with his lips, tasting the sweetness of her skin, savoring the velvet of the tiny hairs.

She sighed and arched to meet him, her hands clenching in his hair. Here was a woman who knew what she wanted and was prepared to take what she liked. The knowledge that she was experienced aroused him further as she planted her feet on the coverlet and let her knees splay. The earthy scent came to him as he tasted her. He moved his fingers and tongue, all to increase her pleasure, savoring the sounds of her growing need.

She spoke to him in a tone husky with passion, encouraging him, saying things he wished were true, calling him her sweetheart, her darling, and when she found her release it was his name she called. He let her rest awhile, using the firm muscle of her thigh as a pillow, drawing what he could not say with his fingertip on her opposite thigh and stomach. Gradually her breathing slowed and then she made a humming sound.

"Come back up here," she said, and he did, gliding along her slick flesh, letting his hips press her down to his bed. He had never brought a woman here, to his home, his refuge, his sanctuary. But it seemed right with Meadow and that troubled him. Getting her here would be easier than convincing her to stay. He almost laughed at the image of her, the party girl, tabloid princess and goat of all goats, living here on the reservation. Riding with him along the river on horseback. Coming to dance when he beat the drum at gatherings.

He could not see any of it.

"That's a serious face," she said.

"Yes, loving a woman is serious business." He had not meant to say it that way. Would she think he meant the act of making love to her? He hoped so. She held her quizzical look for a moment and smiled.

"Why don't you kiss me again?" She lifted her hips and his erection slid along her cleft. The sensation made him suck in a breath.

He kissed her, angling his mouth to show her exactly what he intended to do, his tongue stroking hers in long thrusts. She broke away, whispering against his temple.

"I can't wait. I want to feel you inside me. Dylan, please tell me you've got protection."

He shifted to open the drawer in the bedside table and offered her a foiled condom. She showed strong white teeth as she tore into the packaging, then pushed at his shoulder to encourage him to roll away.

If she wanted to do it, he was willing. Her clever hands stroked down his shaft and before he could make his next move she had straddled him, risen to her knees and then slid down over him. He grasped her hips, setting a pace that was slow and deep. She didn't fight him but whimpered as her fingers curled to rake his chest. The sensations overwhelmed him. He struggled not to finish what they started. But he waited for two reasons. He wanted to watch her ride him, see her body sink down over him with a force that made her lovely full breasts bounce. He didn't know if it was her self-assurance or his passion for this woman that made him so hot, and he didn't care. She was moving faster now, her head thrown back as she took and gave. They seemed to lock in place and then she rose up on her knees again, nearly losing him.

The secret, internal rippling started an instant before she cried out. They rode the wave of ecstasy home together, and then she fell forward to sprawl across his chest, her blue hair rippling down his torso like a wave. He closed his eyes at last, held her there, limp and sated, knowing that he wanted her again, still, forever.

He understood the difference between want and need. His desire for Meadow was too strong to be forgotten or cast aside. That meant that he would need to fight to keep her. Fight her family, his family, his friends and clan and—very possibly—Meadow.

Dylan had never loved a woman before, but he recognized the truth. She had captured him as she had likely done to others before him. He knew he could only keep her if she wanted to be kept.

There was as much chance of stopping a wildfire single-handedly as capturing a woman with a heart as wild as this one's.

MEADOW WOKE WITH a start, not knowing where she was. There, in the dark with her heart hammering, she felt the arms of a man and the familiar scent that reminded her of the one good thing to come out of all this chaos—Dylan.

He drew her in, cradling her against his chest and pressing his lips to her forehead.

"Safe now," he whispered.

She released a breath and felt her racing heart slowing to a strong, steady beat.

"I have you." And here he switched to the language she could not understand.

"What does that mean?"

"Hmm?"

"The words you were saying."

His voice was gravel and slow as if struggling against the grip of a deep sleep.

"Endearments. Like *sweetheart* or *darling*. Literally means…my…heartbeat." His breathing puffed out in a way that told her she had lost him to sleep. But still he held her close, his thumb stroking her shoulder.

His heartbeat? She smiled. What a lovely thing to say.

DYLAN WAS NOT done with her. He knew that her father was not the wealthy philanthropist he pretended to be. Or, if he was this, that was not all he was. That alone was enough to divide them. But there was so much more. He felt the passage of time, the seconds and minutes adding to the moment they would part. If holding her in his arms was enough to keep her here, he would never let go. But soon, very soon, the day would come and the forces of division would appear with the sun.

He closed his eyes, promising himself he would rest only a few moments and knowing from the weariness of his body that he lied. He told himself that she needed some rest before he showed her how much she now meant to him, acted out the devotion and adoration he could not speak aloud.

Once more, he thought, and then once more after that. It would have to be enough. In the end, it was not the sun but those few hours of necessary sleep that stole away his chance to love her again.

Dylan woke to the pounding on his front door.

The gray glow of morning provided enough light for Dylan to recognize Jack Bear Den's white SUV. The words *Tribal Police* were printed across the rear door and back panel in blue lettering, and on the front door was the great seal of the Turquoise Canyon tribe. Detective Bear Den stood on his front step, blocking Dylan's view of the rest of the drive, his arm lifted to beat on the door again.

He flipped open the lock and let in the friend he'd had since grade school. He scrutinized Jack's expression, trying to anticipate the reason for his visit, and thought that the massive man's face seemed thinner, and there were dark smudges under his eyes. Why hadn't he noticed that yesterday? Dylan looked more closely. Was it a trick of the light or the loss of his twin brother that had caused the change in his appearance?

Jack issued a greeting in Tonto Apache.

Dylan returned the greeting. Then he rubbed the palms of his hands into his tired eyes and peered at Jack, studying his posture and expression for clues. He did not like what he saw. Something was wrong.

His thought was that something had happened to Carter, who was now in witness protection, but then he had another thought. It shot through him like an electric current, startling him to alertness. Ray Strong was on the line fighting that fire, the crew chief in his place.

"Ray?"

"No," said Jack, understanding the question, but whether from the panic that must have shown on his face or the tone of his voice, Dylan did not know. "He's fine. Fire is still raging, though. They are hoping the rains will kill it."

"That could be weeks," said Dylan, sick at the possibility that the fire started by a group that purported to protect the environment would burn thousands of acres.

Dylan turned to the next possible reason for his early visit.

"Carter?"

Jack's mouth turned down. "No word."

"Will you come in? I'll make coffee." Dylan hoped he would go away so he could return to his bed and the woman waiting in it.

"I'm sorry, I can't. I need you to come with me."

Dylan's heart cried out as his body braced for some new threat.

"What time is it?"

"Five thirty. Morning paper just arrived. Kenshaw called me. He needs you and the Anglo."

"Her name is Meadow."

"Yes, I know." Jack lifted a folded newspaper and let it drop open so Dylan could read the two-inch-high headline:

Heiress Meadow Wrangler Missing
Casualty or Cause of Fire?

Dylan snatched the paper. The article reported that Meadow had been filming for one of her father's projects when she was caught in the wildfire. Her car had been recovered but no remains. Dylan scanned the article further, seeing that a search was hampered by the active wildfire and road closures. Her father had posted a reward for information.

"They don't know she was in custody?"

"Apparently not," said Jack.

"Twenty-five thousand dollars?" asked Dylan.

"Yup."

"He's after her," said Dylan. "Who saw us come in?"

"Enough people to cause me concern. She can't stay here."

Dylan gripped the door to help him regain control, because his instinct was to fight Jack or anyone else who tried to take Meadow from him.

"Where is Kenshaw?" asked Dylan. Now he needed Tribal Thunder to agree to protect Meadow, an outsider, from her father. That meant convincing their shaman not to let her off the reservation.

"I'll take you to him," said Jack. "He said to hurry. He doesn't have much time."

"He doesn't?" What did that even mean? "Jack, you need to fill me in."

"Can't. Not my place. Get what you need. Pack for traveling."

"What kind of traveling?"

"Unknown. But travel light."

Dylan had the unpleasant task of shaking Meadow out of bed. He paused in the door to his bedroom to try to memorize what she looked like sprawled on his mattress, the covers tangled in her tanned legs and her cobalt-colored hair cascading over his white linen pillowcase. She had one hand raised with curled fingers pressed to her forehead and her mouth was parted as she breathed with slow, even breaths. Her cheeks glowed pink in the rising light and he wondered if that was from the scratch of the stubble on his chin and cheeks. He wanted nothing more than to crawl into bed beside her and love her again.

Instead, he touched her bare shoulder. Her eyes opened and she turned an unfocused gaze on him, casting a sleepy smile.

"Good morning," she said, and then stretched. She sat up and the coverlet dropped away.

His body reacted to the sight of her, naked to the waist. He sucked in a breath as the fire raced through him.

"Come back to bed," she whispered, looping a finger in his boxers and tugging.

He resisted and she frowned.

"Jack's here."

Her finger slipped away and her brow knit. "Here? Why?"

"My shaman has asked to see us right away."

"What's happening?"

Dylan didn't know what was happening or why his shaman needed to see them both right now. He didn't know if he could convince the others of Tribal Thunder to protect Meadow. All he did know was that *he* would protect her. Because over the miles and the minutes, Meadow had risen from responsibility to necessity and Dylan could no longer imagine letting her go.

Chapter Fifteen

Jack Bear Den drove them from Koun'nde. The sun broke over the ridge of pine as they passed the upper ruins. His friend Jack was not good at small talk and Meadow was too worried to be polite so Jack switched to Tonto Apache and spoke to Dylan.

"Is she all right?" asked Jack.

"Afraid of what will happen next. She's been through a lot."

"You both have."

"You really don't know what Kenshaw wants?" asked Dylan.

"I know he sounded out of breath and asked me to meet him in an unusual place. I sent my men first to be sure it was safe for you and the woman."

"Meadow," said Dylan.

She looked at him from the backseat and he smiled, reading concern clearly across her pretty face.

"Yes. Her father is searching for her. You can't keep her a secret for long."

That was true. Most secrets were hard to keep. Jack had secrets, ones he wanted revealed.

"Ray won't be there. Carter, either."

"No. Just you, me and my brother Kurt."

"Have you heard anything from Carter?"

Jack shook his head. "Field Agent Forrest says he's well and they are awaiting the trial to testify."

"Then what?"

"He isn't sure. BEAR is still a credible threat. Carter's wife is the only one who can link Wrangler to the Lilac mine." Jack glanced in the rearview at the woman whose father was the most likely head of BEAR. That made her a threat, too.

"She's not involved."

Jack turned to Dylan. "Oh, no. That's not true. She may be just a pawn or something more. But she is definitely implicated, because someone wanted her killed." They slipped into silence as they reached the Hakathi River and turned toward Piñon Forks.

Jack broke the oppressive stillness first. "I got back the test results on the sibling DNA."

Dylan glanced from the road to Jack. Ray had told him that Carter had complied with Jack's request to take the test. Jack had a theory to explain the fact that he did not resemble his brothers. He thought he had a different father. The simplest way to prove this was to take a sibling DNA test. As Dylan understood it, that was only a swab of the cheek. It would show if you and your sibling shared two parents or only one.

"What did it say?"

"I don't know. I haven't opened it. I carry it around in my wallet. Every day I hold it in my hands and then I put it back."

"But I thought you needed to know."

"I do. But maybe I need not to know more."

Dylan shook his head, not understanding.

"As long as that envelope stays closed, I can pretend…"

As long as the envelope remained closed, then Jack was still Bear Den, still Roadrunner born of Snake, still Tonto Apache. Yes, Dylan understood.

"No hurry, Jack."

Jack met his gaze and smiled.

"I'm with you no matter what you decide." He switched to English. "Hey, have you considered my idea to bring a relay team up to the Brule Sioux Rez? With you as catcher and me as rider, I think we can win." The Indian Relay Races were gaining popularity and he did not want the Sioux to have all the glory.

"The other two?" asked Jack.

"Ray has agreed. I wanted Carter, but if he will not be back by September, maybe Kurt or Tommy," Dylan said, referring to Jack's younger brothers.

"What about Danny?" asked Jack.

"I'll ask Danny. But he won't come home from the rodeo circuit."

"Maybe meet us there?"

"I can ask if you ask Tommy."

"Deal. You really think we can win?"

"Of course."

Jack was smiling again. But he lost his good humor as they pulled into a cutoff leading to a portion of the reservation off-limits to outsiders. This road led to the Turquoise River, one of the few rivers in Arizona that ran year-round, though not as it used to before the series of dams were added in the forties. They were met by a roadblock made of two orange traffic cones and a branch. One of his fellow officers left his unit to greet them.

"They're waiting," said Officer Wetselline. "Chief Tinnin, too."

Jack cursed. If he had hoped to keep something from his boss, Wallace Tinnin, he had failed. None of his force of nine officers moved without him knowing.

Wetselline removed the branch and they rolled past.

Dylan did not know what to expect, but he had packed light, as Jack had requested. He splayed his hand over his duffel and glanced back at Meadow.

"Almost there."

She gave a quick little nod, her brow knitting.

"It will be all right," he said.

Her reply was a wide-eyed expression and clenching jaw that silently relayed she believed it would be anything but.

He turned to Jack. "If we need to make a run for it, will you help us?"

Jack lifted a thick brow. "You'd run, for her?"

Dylan nodded and Jack's expression turned blacker still.

"Yes."

"Mexico?"

"I don't know. I haven't thought it through. Will you?"

Jack nodded. "Hope it doesn't come to that. But yes, I got your back. Always."

They drew up to the lodge and pavilion utilized by the tribe for celebrations and ceremonies. Beyond, a string of cabins sat along the river. Past that, in the trees, was the sweat lodge used by their medicine society, the Turquoise Guardians, and the smaller, elite warrior sect of Tribal Thunder.

Dylan thought he could benefit from a good sweat to remove the poisons of the fire from his body with the ritual cleansing of the sacred sage and cedar smoke. But there was no time. There, in the road beside the pavilion, stood his shaman, the chief of tribal police, Wallace Tinnin, and, beside them, an outsider, FBI field agent Luke Forrest of the Black Mountain Apache Tribe.

"What's he doing here?" asked Dylan.

"Don't know," said Jack. "Nothing good."

"He can't arrest us here. Not on our land."

Jack nodded the truth of that. "But he can arrest her," he said, his chin indicating the passenger in the backseat.

"Jack, you can't let that happen."

His friend lowered his chin, but whether in reply or in preparation for a fight, Dylan did not know. Dylan was always the peacemaker in the group. He'd pulled Ray Strong's fanny from the fire more times than he could count and Jack's, too, on occasion. Now he was the one who was preparing to do something stupid, and he pitied anyone who got between him and Meadow.

"Let's see how this plays out," said Jack, and exited the vehicle.

Dylan glanced to Meadow. "I don't know if you should stay here or..."

Meadow shook her head. "I'm staying with you for as long as I can."

Dylan helped her out and brought her into the

gathering of serious men, all Apache and all dour as
mourners at a funeral. He made introductions.

"Meadow Wrangler, this is my shaman, Kenshaw
Little Falcon."

His shaman did not offer his hand. That was an
Anglo custom and Kenshaw did not believe in such
greetings. He said an open hand was not assurance
that a man did not have a weapon. Kenshaw was the
only one in the bunch without a blazer or sport coat
and looked the least official. His white cotton shirt
covered him from the sun, and the turquoise beads
he always wore fell in heavy cords about his neck.
He looked the elder he was fast becoming because of
his sour expression and the threads of white hairs that
mingled with the black in two straight braids adorned
with nothing more than hair ties. Jeans and boots completed his outfit.

"I know your father," said Kenshaw to Meadow.
"He is a powerful speaker."

Meadow held her smile as she met Wallace Tinnin, who did shake her extended hand and lifted his
drooping features for a moment into a kindly smile
before his face fell back to the perpetual look of a man
on the hunt. He and Luke Forrest both wore their hair
very short and dressed like the Anglos Kenshaw said
they were becoming.

Forrest was Dylan's last introduction. The man was
lean and compact with a power that came from his
bearing as much as his body. Dylan had to resist dragging Meadow behind him when Luke took her hand in
a brief greeting. Suddenly Dylan found himself facing
off against religious, local and federal authorities all

at once. It was a scenario he could not have imagined even three days ago. But so much had changed, and all since he'd met this woman.

"Shall we go into the lodge?" asked Tinnin.

Dylan glanced to Jack, who nodded and then led the way. Inside, they gathered in the office conference area that provided them a wide circular table inlaid with turquoise and set to reveal a spectacular view of the river and the high ridge of gray stone that rose on the opposite bank.

The men waited for Meadow to sit. Dylan flanked one side and Jack took the other. On the opposite side of the table sat Tinnin and Forrest. Little Falcon chose a place between the two parties.

"Why is the FBI here on our land?" asked Dylan.

Kenshaw gave a weary sigh. "Bobcat should be more observant and more patient."

Dylan cautioned himself to patience and stealth. Now more than ever he needed to see what was hidden.

"I am here with my informant," said Forrest.

Dylan looked at Meadow, who met his gaze and then cast him an expression of incredulity peppered with annoyance. Dylan looked from one man to the next. Tinnin could not be an informant, could he? He did not look to Jack, because Jack had no one on whom to inform. In fact, the only one who had access to that kind of information was Little Falcon. But he was their shaman, a religious man who sought to preserve their culture and heritage.

Dylan met Kenshaw's gaze and saw the man's mouth twitch. "Very good, Bobcat."

"You're working with the feds?" Dylan did not manage to keep the distain from his voice.

Once he had thought to join the agency. What had prevented him was the sure knowledge that he would run into conflicts with his people and the mission of the FBI. He wanted to serve his country but balked at being an agent and so had turned down the recruitment that had come after leaving the service and again after Carter Bear Den entered witness protection.

"I have a confession to make to you, Dylan," said Kenshaw. "I did not send you to Cheney Williams for a fire-safety survey for that building site."

Dylan absorbed this blow to his ego and then fielded the curious expression from Jack. Dylan had not told his friend of his intensions to leave the hotshots as crew chief and work in the private sector.

"I was going to tell you," he said to Jack. "I passed the test. I'm accredited now. Ray knows. I just never found the right time."

"Okay. Later," said Jack, and turned to Kenshaw. "So why *did* you send him?"

"Cheney and I were old friends and activists. We worked on the water rights together in the eighties. He and I both joined PAN together."

PAN, Protect All Nature, the environmental group headed by Meadow's oldest brother, a seemingly innocent organization working to preserve wild places. And Cheney Williams had died on that ridge in the explosion that had started the fire that still raged. He had been Kenshaw's friend and he'd worked with Meadow's father on legal matters related to documentary financing and on filing the preliminary injunctions to prevent the building that broke the ridgeline. What else had he been involved in with her dad—the mass shooting in Lilac? Hiring the assassin to kill that shooter?

Cheney was dead. Had Wrangler killed him?

Bobcat waited.

"He and I both joined WOLF in the nineties. I'm still a member." Kenshaw glanced to Forrest who held his expression impassive as he studied Meadow.

"You blew up that dealership in Sedona?" asked Jack.

"Yes." Nothing in Kenshaw's expression or posture held any hint of remorse. But a man had died in that fire. "WOLF targets attacks on groups that encroach on nature."

"Like the first home to break the ridgeline," said Dylan. "Cheney died up there. Was that an accident?"

"I don't think so," said Kenshaw. "I think someone knew he was informing. He was my contact in BEAR. They don't know he was speaking to me."

"How do you know that?" asked Tinnin.

Forrest took that one. "Because he's still alive."

Dylan wondered if he really knew anything about the man who led their warrior sect. Then a more disturbing notion rose to the surface. If Kenshaw worked with WOLF and he controlled Tribal Thunder, then they might have unknowingly done WOLF's bidding.

"I never mixed the two, son." Kenshaw sighed again. "We have to work on that poker face."

Forrest picked up the telling. "Kenshaw has been helping us since Carter Bear Den and Amber Kitcheyan became witnesses."

"Amber Bear Den," corrected Jack. His brother had married Amber, with Kenshaw and Jack as his witnesses, to keep from being separated from Amber when she entered witness protection.

"Yes, right," said Luke. "Kenshaw had foreknowledge of some attack in Lilac." The copper mine was where Ovidio Sanchez had gunned down seven people and then hunted down and shot Amber's boss, narrowly missing Amber.

"But I didn't know what was happening. Only when, so I sent Carter to get my niece."

"Your niece?" asked Luke.

Dylan realized that Field Agent Forrest did not know the family connection between the woman Carter rescued and married and their shaman.

"Amber Kitcheyan Bear Den is the child of my sister, Natalie," said Kenshaw.

Forrest absorbed this. "You should have called the FBI."

"And say what—a friend told me there's going to be trouble in Lilac?"

"Anonymous tip line," said Forrest.

"Ha," said Kenshaw. "Anonymous. That's funny."

Dylan wondered if Kenshaw was working with the FBI only to prevent himself from going to prison. Tinnin and the tribal council could protect him to some extent. They decided which cases to turn over for federal prosecution. Had they turned over Kenshaw?

Police Chief Tinnin brought them back on track. "You were saying?"

"I recommended the man who killed the Lilac Copper Mine mass gunman."

"Morgan Hooke's father," said Dylan. Morgan was the woman Kenshaw had sent Ray Strong to protect. He had done too good a job. Morgan was alive and they were married.

"WOLF had wanted a man with no family, or someone who was terminally ill."

That was the case with Morgan's dad, Dylan knew. He'd had only months to live when he had turned assassin for hire. But his plan to provide for his daughter and granddaughter had backfired and nearly gotten them both killed. Ray had prevented that.

"And that was the last one you set up without us knowing about it," said Forrest.

Dylan thought that sounded more like a warning.

Kenshaw nodded. "Back to Cheney. He was trying to stop that construction with legal action. He needed the fire report to file with the court. I set up the meet so he could get his report and I could get the information he had on BEAR's next target. Cheney said they were planning something big for the explosives they stole from the Lilac mine."

"The house wasn't the target?" asked Meadow.

"My superiors think that the explosion was a warning to others not to break the ridgeline," said Forrest. "And a way to dispose of Cheney."

"What do you think?" asked Meadow.

"It was a test."

A test for what? wondered Dylan. His heart thudded at the possibilities. They had to find out, had to stop BEAR.

Forrest raked his fingers through his thick hair, leaving track marks. "Now we've lost our contact with BEAR. We're blind. We need someone else on the inside."

"Do you know any other members of BEAR?" asked Tinnin.

Kenshaw nodded and looked to Forrest.

"Just one—we suspect he's their leader," said Forrest.

"Who?" asked Jack.

"Meadow's father, Theron Wrangler."

Chapter Sixteen

"No," said Meadow, the outrage shuttering through her voice. "My father would never have set that fire. He's an environmentalist."

"A radical one," said Forrest. "We believe that this explosion was only a test. Cheney had information on the real target. He was supposed to deliver it to Dylan."

Dylan scowled. "It would have been nice if someone had told me that."

"He's fought to protect wild places all his life," she said as the outrage turned to dread. What if they were right?

"Cheney told me that Theron headed BEAR. Theron took over after Walter Fields went to federal prison for manslaughter."

"What did you get him on?" asked Jack.

"Carelessness. He ran down the owner of a fur farm and claimed it was an accident. Jury thought otherwise. Guy had two young kids."

Meadow knew that man. She used to call him Uncle Walt. Now her sense of dread turned to fear. This couldn't be. She would not believe her father could do something like this.

"Why would he endanger his daughter?" said Dylan.

"She broadcast some spectacular footage. It's all over the internet. You've gone viral, Miss Wrangler, and we would very much like to examine that footage more closely. Did anything survive the fire?"

She nodded. "My GoPro."

"Where is it?" asked Forrest.

"I hid it in the gatehouse when those men arrived."

"Where exactly?" asked Forrest.

Meadow described tucking the recorder in between the sheets in the back of the gatehouse's hallway linen closet. Forrest jotted some notes.

"But why her?" asked Dylan. "He could have sent anyone. Why his own daughter?"

"We have a theory," said Forrest.

They waited. Meadow was afraid to breathe.

"Make her a martyr for the cause. The builder had two acetylene tanks on site. The newspapers are theorizing that they blew. The lawsuits are already flying. The builder is facing reckless-endangerment charges. The state sent a fire-and-explosion investigator." He snapped his fingers, thinking. "Albert Waltz. He's on site with our men. We don't believe the tanks were the cause," said Forrest. "They only contributed."

"Do you know what the investigator thinks?" said Dylan.

"He thinks you did it," said Tinnin.

"Why?"

"Means," said Tinnin. "You know how to weld. Learned in the Marines, and you picked up a few jobs here, too. Motive. You're Apache and everyone knows we are opposed to assaults on the environment."

"That's weak," said Jack.

Tinnin went on as if his detective had not spoken. "Opportunity. You were there when it blew and yet somehow miraculously survived."

"It wasn't a miracle. I deployed a fire shelter."

"Which you happened to have along," said Forrest.

"I always do."

"Most folks don't carry them," countered Forrest.

"Most folks aren't hotshots."

"All right," said Tinnin. "Point being, that explosives guy, Waltz, is going to arrest you the minute you leave the reservation."

Meadow's anxiety switched from her father to Dylan.

"He didn't do it."

The chief of tribal police gave her an indulgent smile. "That likely won't matter. Waltz has a warrant and has applied to the tribal council for Dylan's release to his custody, which they won't accommodate. Makes him a prisoner here, though."

"Only way around that is to clear his name," said Jack.

And that meant getting Waltz a new suspect—her father, she realized.

"My video!"

"It shows me heading to the site," said Dylan.

"And coming back. You didn't have time," she said.

"Could have done it earlier," said Jack.

"We need to see that footage," said Forrest. "Excuse me." He stepped away to make a call.

"His partner is at the epicenter," said Tinnin. "With that inspector, Waltz."

Forrest returned to the table and spoke to Meadow. "Can you tell me what you shot?"

She gave him a summary. She'd filmed the ridge before construction and then the house in various stages of development.

"Oh, there's other footage on there, too. Unrelated. I'm working on two projects."

Forrest quirked a brow. "What's the other?"

"A documentary—in its early stages—on the effect of damming the Hakathi River. They modified it to prevent floods and generate hydroelectric power. But they changed it irrevocably."

"What did you film?" asked Jack.

"The power company gave us permission to film the exteriors of all four dams and I got some interior shots at the Skeleton Cliff and Alchesay Canyon Dams. Those guys up there were really friendly. Even took me in a crane basket for some of my footage."

Jack straightened and Forrest met his gaze. They both looked to Kenshaw.

"Maybe," he said.

They didn't like that information. Meadow waited for someone to speak. Instead, their shaman motioned for her to continue. So she described the footage she had taken.

"The inside of the powerhouse isn't very cinematographic, just cooling turbines and sluice gates to control water flow and a lot of compressed air in big tanks. That's on there, too. Just in between the ridge footage."

"You stream any of that?" asked Forrest.

"No. It's for research on the next project. Nice guys up there, the engineers."

Dylan said something to Detective Bear Den in Tonto Apache and the detective shook his head and replied, looking to Forrest. The next thing Dylan said was a question. She could tell that much.

"Skeleton Cliff is right above our reservation," Dylan said in English. "It will be at capacity after the summer rains."

He'd gone pale. Meadow recalled the ridge explosion and suddenly felt sick. If the dams were the real target, the target Cheney would have revealed to the shaman through Dylan, then his tribe, his people, his home—everything and everyone in his entire world would be washed away if Skeleton Dam failed.

"What do you mean?" asked Meadow.

Dylan shook his head as if words just failed him.

"My father didn't blow up that house. Neither did Dylan," said Meadow to the FBI agent.

"Well, if you really believe that, then you'll want to clear your father," said Forrest. "You'll want to help us out with the investigation."

Meadow hesitated. Her actions could incriminate her father. What would she do if it became a choice between her father and the man who had saved her life? Meadow prayed she would never have to make that choice.

"I won't do anything to incriminate my father."

"We just want the truth, Meadow. We all want the truth."

"What is it you want her to do, exactly?" asked Dylan.

Forrest switched his attention to Dylan. "We want her to go home."

"That's it?" said Meadow. Some of the tension eased from between her shoulders.

"And wear a wire."

Her muscles tensed again. A wire? Like those things she saw on TV. She'd then be some kind of family narc. How had her life become a crime drama? Forrest's phone chirped and he glanced down at the screen.

"We have your camera," he said to Meadow. "Thank you for providing us the location. We'll make a copy of the footage for you and get the hardware back to you soon."

Meadow snorted as if she doubted that and stuck to the topic of the wire.

"You want me to be an informant against my father."

"We want you to prove us wrong."

She wasn't falling for that bait.

"What if I don't?"

"Nothing. You can go home, alone, without FBI protection to your loving family."

Meadow glanced to Dylan.

"Oh, he stays here. He leaves, he loses tribal protection. Remember?" said Forrest.

Dylan placed his arm across the table, a visible barrier between Meadow and Forrest, just to let Forrest know he wouldn't let her go without a fight.

"She stays here," said Dylan.

"No. Whether or not she cooperates, I'm placing her into custody. Whether that becomes public knowledge is also up to Miss Wrangler. Of course, I could arrange for Waltz to back off for a while."

Meadow understood the threat. If she cooperated and wore a wire like a good girl, she'd get Dylan and the FBI's protection. Refuse, and she'd be left alone and everyone would know she'd been detained by the FBI—everyone, including her father. Meadow rubbed her hand over her mouth as she considered her options.

"Don't, Meadow," said Dylan. "It's too dangerous."

But it was also a chance to clear Dylan's name and, if she was right, her father's, as well.

"Under the condition that you get Dylan cleared of charges before we leave the reservation."

"I can't clear him. I can only buy him time."

"But you know he didn't do it."

Forrest leaned in. "You don't get it, do you, Meadow? I don't care who did it. I want to know who has the rest of those explosives and where they plan to strike next. Someone out there has dump trucks full of explosives and a moral obligation to send the entire Southwest back into the Stone Age. That's not happening. Not on my watch. So you can help me or you can watch it happen."

"Okay," she said. "I'll do it."

DYLAN DID NOT like the plan, but he waited as Meadow was outfitted with a wire, and then he stood placidly as Forrest applied one to him, as well.

When she returned, she was given a burner phone to call her father. Dylan listened on headphones with the rest of them. He picked up on the first ring, his greeting taciturn.

"Yeah?"

"Daddy?"

Everything in his voice changed. "Princess. Is it you? I knew it. Oh, baby, are you all right? Where are you?"

If he was acting, it was darn convincing. Dylan read only relief and joy in Theron Wrangler's voice.

"I'm okay. I'm sorry if I worried you. I only just got the phone replaced."

"They found your car. But not you… Sweetheart, what happened?"

She relayed the lie as it had been set up.

"I got out before the fire. Some guy picked me up and we just made it out."

"Thank God. Thank God." He was mumbling to himself now. "I knew… I just knew it." There was a choking sound.

"Daddy?" Meadow's eyes rounded as she listened to her father weep. She held Dylan's gaze and he saw her eyes fill with tears. "Daddy? I'm sorry. I should have called right away."

"I'm so glad you're safe."

Dylan thought again that this did not sound like a man willing to martyr his daughter for the cause. But if he was not the one, then who?

"You need to come home," he said. "Tell me where you are."

"I'm in Darabee."

"Darabee? In the mountains?"

"Yes. The guy that got me out, he lives up here. I

lost my phone and my wallet and everything but the camera. Did you see the footage, Dad?"

"The hell with the footage. I'm sending Jessie to pick you up. They have a small airport. Can you get there?"

"Yes. Daddy, can I bring him?"

"Who?"

"The man who saved my life."

"Heck, yes. I want to meet that young man."

She lowered her voice. "Daddy, he's Apache, from the Turquoise Canyon tribe."

Dylan's eyes narrowed at the long pause.

"Apache? That's a heck of a thing. What's his name?"

His tone had changed now, seemingly casual but with a hard undercurrent that Jack and Luke also caught because their eyes flashed to him and then each other.

"Dylan Tehauno. He's wonderful."

"Sure he is. He's a hero. Saved my baby girl. Tell him there's a reward in it for him."

"He doesn't want money, Daddy." Her face wrinkled in disapproval and she shot Dylan an apologetic look.

"Well, what does he want?"

"Nothing."

"Hmm." Dad had been around long enough to know that everyone wanted something, and if it wasn't money it was something worse. "A job?"

"No. Daddy, we're dating."

Another long pause. "I don't think so."

"What?" Her expression read absolute disbelief.

"You're not dating a boy from the rez."

"He's a man."

"Without a job, likely, who latched on to the best thing that ever came his way."

"I'd better go," she said.

"I'm sending Jessie."

"Don't bother. I'll find my own way home."

Forrest was waving at her as Meadow went off script.

Silence stretched as Meadow affected a look of petulance Dylan had never seen. The grit and intelligence of this woman dissolved as she reverted into a child on the verge of a tantrum.

"All right," said Wrangler.

Meadow's mouth curled in a smile. The victor, Dylan realized.

Wrangler continued, conceding. "He can come. But do not introduce him to your mother as your newest flame. She won't have it. You know that."

"She doesn't have to date him."

"You need her approval."

"Only if I want a wedding with five hundred people."

"Wedding! Princess, we need to talk."

Dylan's eyes widened at this turn and his gaze flashed to Jack, who was now scowling. Dylan shook his head, wondering what game Meadow was playing.

"Isn't that what we're doing?" asked Meadow.

"Have you met his family?"

"Some," she lied.

"Did you meet a man named Little Falcon up there?"

"No. Just his mother. She's lovely. Very gracious

and welcoming. She didn't seem to mind that I was a white girl."

"Of course she didn't. I'm sending Jessie. Get to the airport."

"With Dylan."

"Great." His voice belied his words.

"Love you, Daddy."

"Oh, Princess, I am so damn glad you are alive."

"See you soon." She disconnected.

Forrest slumped in his chair. Jack shook his head in disbelief, and Dylan wondered if he was as easily manipulated as her father.

"What?" she said.

"You're used to getting your way," said Dylan.

"With Daddy, yes. But Mom is tougher." Meadow tucked away her new smartphone in the pink sparkle case. "She's very hard to please."

Was that why she'd given up trying, playing the family screwup, instead. Any attention was better than no attention after all.

"I'm sorry," said Dylan.

"About what?"

"Your mom."

"Yeah, well, you'll be sorrier after you meet her. She's going to eat you for lunch and send me to a nunnery."

"She doesn't like Apache Indians."

"She likes professional men with their own money. You got any money, Dylan?"

"I got this?" he said, lifting the choker of silver and turquoise beads that ringed his neck. "And a claim from my grandfather to get more of the same."

She hugged him tight. "This will be hard. I don't usually bring a man home unless I want to get a rise out of her."

"She'll think I'm there to upset her, then."

"Probably."

"I can play that part. Might enjoy it."

"You won't," she whispered.

Dylan lowered his chin and she lifted up to kiss him. Suddenly the danger they faced slipped away in a haze of desire.

Forrest cleared his throat. Dylan broke away and cast him an impatient look.

"We have to get you two over to the airport."

"I'll drive them," said Jack.

"We've got a team in Phoenix. They are in position to surveil and assist, if necessary. Just use the code word and we'll pick you up."

Destiny, he recalled. That sent the FBI into attack mode. He hoped he wouldn't need it. But if they were right, he and Meadow were flying into a lion's den.

Chapter Seventeen

Meadow pressed her hand over the wire that had been affixed between her breasts with paper tape. The helicopter blades made any conversation impossible, and anything she said into the headset was also heard by Jessie. She felt as if she had dropped down the rabbit hole. Everything seemed familiar but changed when, in truth, only she had changed.

The suspicion tainted everything. As the runners touched down she spotted her father's Mercedes sedan, big and white and pretentious. He had a Jeep and a Range Rover and also the Ferrari. The Mercedes was the vehicle her mother used for impressing potential donors to PAN and meetings with film producers. She swallowed her dread at the possibility that her mother was waiting behind those tinted windows.

The blades slowed and Dylan touched her wrist and shook his head, glancing at her chest. She dropped her hand. The involuntary action, touching the wire, could get them both killed—if the FBI was right about her father.

Were they?

The FBI said her father was the head of BEAR.

Could he head an organization so violent and that had such a bleak outlook on the human condition that they called for a do-over? One that did not include people. They did not just incidentally kill people while protecting the natural world. According to Forrest, they encouraged it.

And the FBI really believed that her father had sent her up there, to the mountains outside Flagstaff, to die.

Her father stepped from his vehicle, his salt-and-pepper hair blowing in the artificial wind of the slowing chopper blades. His hair had once been the same soft brown color as hers. Her brothers and sisters had inherited the thick black hair of their mother, and her deep brown eyes. Her mother didn't like Meadow's hair, calling it mousy brown. It was one of the reason she'd died it ocean blue. Not surprisingly, her mother had not liked that any better.

Their eyes met and he smiled, flashing white teeth that now looked dangerous in their brightness. He extended his arms in welcome and she forced down her apprehension. This was her dad, the one who always indulged and pampered her to the point that her brothers' and sisters' jealousy hardened into disdain and disapproval. Only Katrina managed to look past her favored status and keep their relationship alive.

When would she grow up? When would she do something with her life?

Her brother Miguel's lecture ran in a loop in her mind. Well, she had grown up, suddenly and all at once, in that fire shelter when the man beside her had used his body to protect hers. She had come to appreciate her life and found her purpose. She wanted to know the truth, and she was willing to do whatever was necessary to discover who had sent her to die.

She was here to prove her father guilty or innocent, and she really, truly, did not know which he was. Her heart prayed for innocence as her mind spouted facts. He had asked her to film that day. He had sent her up there. Him.

Jessie stepped out first. She waited for him to open her door and then climbed down, keeping low.

"Princess Meadow!" called her father, and met her halfway. He enfolded her in his arms, squeezing so tight she could not breathe. Did he feel the transmitter taped to her torso? "I'm so happy to have you home."

He kissed her forehead and she pulled away. Dylan was out of the chopper.

She slipped naturally under her father's arm and motioned to Dylan. His transmitter was inside his truck's key fob, which had been clipped to the loop of his jeans.

"Daddy, this is my hero, Dylan Tehauno of the Bear Clan."

The minute she said "bear" her heart skipped. Her father's arm tightened and then he stepped away to shake Dylan's hand.

"Bear, huh?" he asked.

"Bear born of Butterfly. My tribe is Turquoise Canyon."

"Beautiful country, except for the river. They've ruined that, the salmon runs, the migrations."

"Yes, sir."

"Well, I want to thank you for getting my girl out of the fire. I'm in your debt, Mr. Tehauno."

"My pleasure."

Her father's smile hardened. Their hands remained clasped a beat too long as the men sized up each other. Her father's smile reemerged as he dropped his hand and returned to her side.

"Well, we need to get you home, Princess." He gave her a squeeze. "Can we drop you somewhere, Mr. Tehauno?"

Dylan's gaze flicked to her.

"That's not funny, Daddy."

Her father's smile held, but his eyes stayed pinned on Dylan. He didn't like her new beau and it wasn't really a joke. He looked like he would love to drop him somewhere. That was certain.

"In we go." He motioned to his limo and the man in uniform who held open the back door.

"Where's Mom?" asked Meadow, feeling both relieved and disappointed her mother had not come to greet her.

"She's working, Princess. But we'll see her tonight. Big welcome-home dinner just for you. Your brothers and sisters will be there, and some of your friends."

Dylan wondered if that might be worse than confronting the man. As it turned out, he would have been happier battling a wildfire on the line with Ray. At least then he would have had a clear escape route.

Dylan remained silent as Wrangler and Meadow conversed about the revised version of events since she had left to film.

"What about the camera?" asked her father.

Meadow looked away to lie. "Gone."

"Well, no matter. Great footage. Best you ever shot."

And it had nearly killed her. Dylan felt sick as he saw Meadow beam with pride. They used the highway to circle the outskirts of Phoenix and then headed up into the gated luxury communities that lay south of the city in the pine forest and mountain meadows. The Wranglers' home sat on a golf course, which Dylan found ironic. The log-and-stone exterior included a huge portico, where they were greeted by staff. Dylan trailed behind Wrangler, who looped his arm in Meadow's as they strolled through a home larger than his tribe's headquarters. The interior was rich with polished wood, flagstone and wrought iron. Sculptural glass pieces filled niches above the fireplace, and he spotted a beautiful Navajo rug draped over a leather couch that looked as if no one ever sat on it.

In the back of the house, between the golf course and the huge outdoor seating area was a lap pool. It was there he met her mother, who had been "working" on her tan.

Lupe Wrangler floated on a pink raft in the shallow end in a two-piece neon-orange suit that showed a full figure. Her raven hair was pulled into a ponytail that fell over the visor shading her eyes and onto the headrest of the float. Mrs. Wrangler did not bother to leave the pool as they appeared but paddled to the stairs, where she stood in knee-deep water to meet Meadow with a perfunctory kiss, accompanied by a cutting comment that she still smelled of wood smoke. Likely, Dylan thought, from the fire in the tribe's meeting house. She did not bother to greet Dylan but lowered her glasses down her nose to stare.

"So this is the latest. Interesting choice." The

glasses slid back into place. The woman exited the pool and dragged on a sheer cover-up that did little to hide the neon-orange bikini beneath. Her dark skin came either from her lineage or a dedication to tanning. With her black hair and deep brown eyes, she did not look like the mother of the fair-skinned Meadow. Suspicions rose immediately in Dylan's mind.

Meadow resembled her father, Dylan realized, and perhaps someone else?

"Your father insisted on a party," said Lupe Wrangler. "I told him that the less attention we draw, the better. But you know your father."

Dylan watched as Meadow's smile became brittle and her eyes glassy. Lupe sank into her lounge chair with her drink. She did not offer her daughter or her guest a drink or ask them to join her. It made him think of the adage his grandmother often repeated: *Assume that your guests are tired and hungry and act accordingly.*

"You'll want to clean up and dress before dinner," said Lupe, lifting a magazine.

Meadow remained where she was. Her mother glanced at her and a raven brow lifted above the tops of her sunglasses.

"Well?"

"This man saved my life, Mother. He's not an interesting choice. He's a hero."

Her mother frowned. "Don't be dramatic, dear. Your father told me all about it. All he did was stop to pick you up. Anyone would have done the same."

Not here, Dylan thought. She'd have driven right

by Meadow. Maybe over her. Was she intentionally trying to be cruel?

Lupe flipped the pages of her magazine, dismissing her daughter and ending the conversation.

Meadow's face reddened but she said nothing, just turned and retreated into the house.

Her father waited there, arms folded as he watched the exchange.

"She was worried about you," he said.

"Yes. I can see that. Did she miss a manicure waiting for news?"

Her father's smile seemed sad to Dylan. Lupe Wrangler was beautiful and cold as an ice sculpture.

Theron walked them through the foyer, the polished wood tile echoing with their steps.

"Guests are arriving at eight. That will give you some time to rest. Have a swim."

Dylan thought of swimming in front of the ice queen and found the prospect left him cold.

"If you need anything, Mr. Tehauno, please just ask—something more appropriate for dinner, perhaps?"

Dylan gave a half smile. "I'll be wearing this." He plucked at his cotton shirt, causing the heavy multistrand necklace of turquoise mingled with silver beads to thump against his chest.

"Of course."

Meadow took him upstairs, and they spent the afternoon resting in her suite of rooms. The sitting room and bedroom looked like a magazine spread but nothing like a home. Meadow selected a silver dress from her cavernous closet and tossed it on the bed. Then she slipped out of the shirt he had given her and into the metallic sheath, transforming before his eyes from the woman he had come to know to the party girl she had claimed to be. The low-cut cocktail dress accentuated her slim figure and revealed her long legs. He wondered if the dress was selected specifically to irritate her mother. She applied a generous coating of makeup, a red lipstick and silver earrings that brushed her shoulders. She waited until eight thirty to leave her bedroom suite. One of the waitstaff stood holding a necktie and blazer out for Dylan. He accepted the jacket and refused the tie. Together he and Meadow descended the grand staircase with her arm in the crook of his elbow. Meeting the guests, Dylan felt as out of place as a fish in the Mojave Desert.

Her friends were all Anglo, well-educated and oh-so-careful to appear socially conscious and forward thinking as they surreptitiously checked their text messages every few minutes. Her brother Phillip was short and fat and old enough to be Meadow's father. Dylan found him to be a blowhard and his handshake seemed to be compensating for something. He let Dylan know how important he was by spouting statistics like a whale spouts water as he yakked about their operating budget, his staff and the very necessary efforts and successes PAN had managed as cocktails were served and appetizers offered by the waitstaff.

He was seated for dinner between Katrina and Rosalie, Meadow's attorney sisters, who interrogated him like a witness to a crime, and so far across the enormous table that he could not touch or speak to Meadow. Dessert was served in another room entirely but at least he could leave the witness chair and return to Meadow. As the evening dragged along, her friends grew louder and her mother more catty. Lupe Wrangler cornered him in the dining room after dinner.

"You won't have her for long. No one does."

"Thanks for the warning."

"You must think you died and went to heaven." She swept her hand about in the air, indicating the opulence all about them.

"Should I?"

"Of course. I've visited some of Arizona's reservations. Garbage everywhere, filthy little hovels of houses. The government should be ashamed."

"Should they?"

"I think so. I don't know why you don't rise up against them."

"We tried that in the 1870s. Didn't work out."

Her lips curled in a mirthless smile.

"Well, you're more interesting than her usual fare, I'll give you that. My girls tell me you fight wildfires."

The gathered intelligence had already been received, he thought.

"Yes. I'm with the Turquoise Canyon Hotshots."

"Do you ever think that fire is nature's way of cleaning the palate?"

"I've heard that argument. But nature doesn't start most of the fires I fight. Men do."

Her smile never faltered as she inclined her head as if giving him a point. Catlike eyes regarded him then swept away.

"It's mine, you know?" she said, surveying her home over the rim of her glass. "My husband is a self-made man, but he was wise enough to marry money. *My* money."

"Good to know." Dylan glanced around for rescue.

"Dirty money mostly," said Lupe. "Great-Granddad had oil-drilling companies in Mexico before they nationalized. My grandfather built offshore drilling platforms for the Mexican government. One of them had a blowout and the oil ignited. Massive spill in 1979." She paused and lifted her brows expectantly.

He shook his head.

"Too young to recall it, then. Wish I was, but time marches on." She stroked her hand under her jaw as if judging the texture of her skin. "I don't do anything much except invest in my husband's films and follow the golden rule, Don't Touch the Principal."

Dylan thought he understood why Lupe might marry a man with an environmental agenda. She had a family legacy that would give anyone pause. He looked about for Meadow, but she was nowhere in sight.

"Do you know Kenshaw Little Falcon?"

"Yes." He tried not to tense.

"He did some good work stopping the land swaps. We couldn't have prevented that Canadian mining company from coming in here if not for the efforts of the Turquoise Canyon and Black Mountain tribes. I hear he's negotiating the water rights up there in Turquoise Canyon."

"He's very active in a number of worthy causes."

"He came down here to protest that house breaking the ridgeline. Did you know that?"

"I did not."

"What do you think about the encroachment of housing into wild places?"

Meadow rescued him. Her mother's expression went sour the instant she spotted her youngest.

"Here she comes. The prodigal child returns." She slipped an arm around Meadow and gave her shoulder a little pat. Then she leaned in and whispered, "What are you wearing?"

Meadow ignored her. "I'm going to steal Dylan. I want him to meet my friend Veronica."

Her mother waved her away.

"Sorry about that," said Meadow. She steered them up the stairs to the balcony over the portico. The breeze was absent and the night so much hotter than up in his mountains. They looked out at the city of Phoenix twinkling in the distance.

"Do you want me to meet your friend?"

"Not really. But you will. My friends are all curious about you."

They had only a few minutes of peace before Rosalie and Katrina found them and the interrogation resumed. If he did not know, he would not have guessed these two were Meadow's sisters because she was taller, lighter in skin tone and a completely different body type. Where Meadow's frame was model thin, her sisters had full figures and wore clothing that hugged those curves and revealed enough cleavage to make a man lose his concentration. They were short, and even the high-heeled sandals did not bring them eye level with their youngest sister.

He tried to ask Rosalie about the projects she oversaw at PAN and to discover what kind of fund-raising

Katrina organized for her parent's upcoming release, but they carefully steered all conversation to his rescue of Meadow and his work with the hotshots. They barely acknowledged their little sister. When they finally glided away on four-inch heels he felt as if he'd just survived running the rapids on the Snake River.

He blew out a breath.

"That goes double for me," she said. "Want something to drink?"

"Water with lemon." He didn't drink and, though tempting, he wasn't starting now when he was in a nest of vipers.

Meadow flagged a waiter, who returned a few moments later with two drinks on a silver tray. Meadow lifted the wine, swirling the burgundy liquid before taking a long swallow. He took a large gulp from his drink and found it tasted of chemicals. He grimaced and set the tumbler aside. Meadow had already finished her drink and signaled for another.

"Bad idea," he said.

"Two-glass limit. Also, my mother hates it when I drink."

They had a few minutes alone as Meadow nursed her second glass of wine. Then she made her excuses to her mother and kissed her father, then led him to the room he would use while under her parents' roof. It was too far from Meadow, so he followed her back to her room.

"My head aches," she said, her words slurred.

He'd been battling an upset stomach since just after dinner.

"Did you have anything else to drink?" he asked.

"Two glasses. That's it." She blinked slowly and her lids remained half-closed.

His stomach pains escalated. Dylan spoke so that FBI field agents Forrest and Cosen could hear.

"I think we've been drugged. Meadow is blacking out. I've got stomach pains. Destiny. Destiny," he said, repeating the code for help.

"What?" she said, her eyes widening.

Dylan wasn't taking chances. He lifted the phone on her desk and got no dial tone.

"Cell phone?" he said, wanting to call Jack.

She motioned at her satiny silver cocktail dress. "Don't have it."

He lifted her by the shoulders and took her to her bathroom. There he told her to make herself vomit. He did the same. But it was too late for Meadow. She was already dropping into a drug-induced slumber. He lifted her, determined to take her out of this house. He got his arms under her legs and lifted, but she was so heavy. Instead of bringing her up into his arms, he fell to his knees on the bathroom floor.

"Forrest," he said. "Help."

Had the agents heard them?

The door to her room banged open. Dylan managed to get one knee under him. His vision was bad and the two men seemed a blur of motion, coming at him too fast for him to react.

"This one's still conscious," said the one in blue.

"Knock him out, then check him for a wire."

Dylan roared and lunged. He caught the one in blue around the waist and drove him through the doorway and knocking him to his back. The jolt of their landing made his head pound, but he lifted a fist to finish the job. Something heavy hit him in the back of the head so hard he saw stars. The wide wood-floor planking rushed up to greet him. He tried to rise and someone hit him again.

Chapter Eighteen

Meadow woke to the smell of smoke and a stomach that heaved with every jolt. She'd had her fair share of hangovers—okay, more than her fair share. And she'd woken up in some unexpected places. But she didn't do that anymore.

Why not?

Then she remembered. Dylan Tehauno. Since she had met him she had lost much of her inclination toward reckless self-destruction.

The car hit another jolt and she groaned.

"Sleeping Beauty is waking up."

She knew that voice.

"Won't matter. We're here."

The car pulled to a stop, bumping along on uneven ground.

Meadow could not get her eyes to stay open. It took all her effort just to lift her lids a slit as the door beside her head swung out. She was hauled from the vehicle by her wrists. Her legs banged into the wheel well and then onto the ground. Next, her heels dug twin trenches in the sand. She managed a sound that was more mew than cry.

"Jeez, I can barely see through the smoke," said the first man.

Who was that?

She was dropped unceremoniously on the ground. Her cheek hit hard and the sharp sting of pain helped rouse her. She opened her eyes and saw yellow grass and two legs clad in gray trousers. Either the light was bad or it was her vision. Was it still evening or early morning?

"Come on. Let's get him and then get them both into the house."

Him? Were they talking about Dylan?

"What'd you give the guy at the roadblock?"

The other man snorted. "Money. They evacuated this neighborhood yesterday. Wrangler says it's a goner. Smoke should kill them even before the fire gets here. Either way, we'll be on our way back to Phoenix."

She did cry out this time.

"You hear that, Princess? Should have died up here the first time. You recognize it? The ridge fire outside Flagstaff? Welcome back."

She tried and failed to roll to her back. What had they given her? It was like she was paralyzed, unable to get her body to listen to the commands of her mind.

They walked past her and then returned, dragging Dylan. They dropped him on his back beside her. His head lolled and she saw the drying blood that had run across his forehead and into his eyes. He didn't move, and for a moment she thought they had killed him. But then she saw it—the blood leaking from a wound on the back of his head. Dead men didn't bleed, did they?

Really, she didn't know.

"Dylan," she cried, her words only a whisper.

He remained completely still. Tears leaked from her eyes. This was her fault. She'd wanted to prove her father's innocence, and Dylan wouldn't have let her go alone. She didn't care if she had to join the 27 Club if only she could save Dylan. He was so much better than her in every way imaginable. And she loved him.

The tears now choked her as she admitted the truth. She loved him and it was going to get him killed.

Beyond her tiny view of the world, she heard the sound of a motor and the clang of metal. The men returned.

"Is he alive?" she asked.

"Not for long," said her captor, and then she knew him. It was Joe Rhodes, one of the soundmen on her father's documentary projects.

"Joe. Don't do this."

"I'd say sorry, but I'm not. You cannot believe what I'm getting for this." He scooped her up and then carried her from her resting place, past the truck and up a driveway made of paver stone. She controlled her head, but the rest of her body did not seem attached. Her legs swung and her arms dangled. She couldn't really feel them. When Joe passed the driveway and carried her around toward the back of the large ornate Spanish-style home, the smoke came directly at them, a hot rush of air, like the kind from a blast furnace used to fuse glass. The skin on her face tingled.

"Why?" she asked Joe.

"Wrangler's orders. I guess someone is tired of cleaning up after your messes. I would have put you over my knee about twenty years ago. Someone should have. But they never cared enough about you to do that. Did they, Princess?"

Joe shifted her over his shoulder to maneuver through a wrought-iron gate and then draped her across a lounge chair with what should have been a fine view of the ridgeline. Instead, it gave her a horrific picture of the approaching line of orange flames that would soon overtake this home.

Joe left her. She screamed at him to come back and choked on the acrid smoke. Seconds ticked by as she tried to get just her little finger to move. The gate creaked open and then banged shut. The next time she heard the gate, Joe and the second man had returned carrying Dylan between them. She now recognized the second guy, as well. Mark Perkinson, her sister Rosalie's legal assistant. He leaned down and stroked her cheek.

"Just drop him here," said Joe, releasing Dylan's knees. Mark grunted and then lowered Dylan to the flagstone patio. Mark approached and stood over her, hands on hips.

"Not too good for me now, are you?"

She vaguely recalled turning him down at a holiday party some years ago.

"Mark. You have to help us."

Mark turned to Joe. "She's talking. I thought she'd be out the whole time."

"So hit her on the head," said Joe.

"She's not a catfish," said Mark.

"But she's going to fry like one," said Joe, and

snorted at his joke. Then he turned toward the gate. "Come on. We don't want to get trapped up here, too."

"Should we put the camera near them so it looks like they were filming the fire?" asked Mark.

"Just set it up." Joe's coughing was worse. "Then turn it on."

"Why on? It's just going to burn up."

"I don't know. Wrangler wants it on."

There it was again. Wrangler. She squeezed her eyes shut against the stinging smoke as her heart split in two. Her father had done this to her. He was exactly what the FBI had told her, a madman, an extremist bent on returning the earth to pristine glory before humans interfered.

She did not know what her death would achieve. Perhaps she would be a martyr for his cause.

Then she had a thought. The wire. The FBI. They'd be listening. They'd know where to find them.

But then why hadn't they come already?

She looked down at her dress and found the back zipper open so the low neckline gaped. The skin between the pink cups of her bra was bare. The wire was gone.

"She's moving," said Perkinson.

The wire…was gone. They were on their own and no one knew where to find them.

"Won't matter. Come on." Joe disappeared and she heard the gate creak. Mark spared her a backward glance.

"Sorry," he muttered, and followed Joe.

Meadow rolled her head back to the approaching wall of flames, the pungent stench of charring

wood now hauntingly familiar. Death was coming
for her and she was filled with regrets, so many they
ate away at her like termites in rotting wood. Even
as the smoke stung her eyes, she came to a certain
clarity that Dylan was the one good thing in her life.
He had treated her with the respect and tenderness
that was absent in her family. Why did her father
want her dead?

They had always been so close. He had never denied her anything and that had been a constant source
of contention between her parents. Her mother could
not and would not approve of her lifestyle or her ac-
complishments, few as they were.

Up on the ridge, the dry piñon trees had no chance
against the fire that consumed them, crackling through
their branches and turning the crowns into torches.
Behind the flames lay a hillside of blackened earth.

Why weren't their firefighters here trying to save
this neighborhood? She tried to think. Sometimes the
fire teams deemed an area unsalvageable and offered
it as sacrifice to the gods of fire. That would please
her parents because she knew how her mother and
father felt about the overdevelopment in this canyon.
Though they didn't object to their own older gated
community and the golf course that sucked up pre-
cious water.

Meadow reached out and clasped Dylan's limp
hand and squeezed. He did not move. She looked at
her hand clutching his and realized she had moved
her hand.

What would Dylan do?

She didn't know, but she was sure that he would

not be mourning a misspent youth. He'd be fighting for their lives. And that was exactly what she intended to do.

Chapter Nineteen

Someone was calling his name from a long way off. Dylan roused to the feeling that his head had been cracked open like a goose egg. He squeezed his eyes shut, smelling smoke and blood. He lifted a hand to wipe away the sticky fluid pooling in his eye sockets and then moved his fingers beneath his nose to smell the drying blood. His fingers then raked through his hair to the gash that sat on a lump at the back of his skull.

"Don't touch it. It's still bleeding."

He blinked open his eyes to see Meadow kneeling beside him, her features tight with worry as her amber eyes met his.

Dylan registered the unmistakable smell of a wildfire and looked about.

"Where are we?"

"Back at the ridge fire. Two of my father's men dropped us here."

"Why?"

"I think they'd like us to die."

Dylan swung his legs off the padded lounge chair and onto the flagstone. Meadow still wore the pretty satin cocktail dress she'd had on last night and he was still in his clothing, necklace plus the borrowed blazer. His shirt had been opened and the wire that had been affixed to his chest had been removed.

"Someone hit me from behind. Twice." He grappled with the pain and dizziness that came with each tiny movement.

"I was drugged. I couldn't even move until a few minutes ago. It was like some nerve toxin."

Dylan looked at the line of fire rushing down the hillside in their direction. They had to get out of here.

"Have you tried the phones inside?" he asked.

She shook her head. Dylan opened the locked glass sliders by using the base of the wrought-iron side table as a battering ram. The force needed to shatter the glass made his eyes water as the pain flipped the contents of his stomach. His coordination was dismal as he staggered inside the ornate dining room using the upholstered chair backs for support. In the kitchen, Meadow found a phone on the wide expanse of black honed granite. She lifted the handset and pressed the call button. She gripped the counter with her opposite hand and swayed as if she stood on a ship's deck in rough seas. What had they given her?

"No service," she said, her words slower than usual. She squeezed her eyes shut and gave her head a shake.

He reached her and drew her close.

"We have to go," he said. Maybe the residents had left a car in the garage. He wouldn't have. If he'd had two cars and this house, he would have loaded up everything he could carry and left when the evacuation was called. Still, they stumbled to the garage and found the three bays empty except for a golf cart.

She looked at him and he made a face.

"Terrible escape vehicle," he said, glancing at the open sides.

"It's that or the bikes," she said, motioning to the expensive mountain bikes neatly stored on hooks beside the ski equipment and golf clubs. "And my balance is off."

He took her arm and guided her to the cart, where they found the ignition key missing. A search of the tiny glove box, cup holders and beneath the seats yielded nothing.

"I'll bet it's on his key chain."

"Hot-wire," he said.

Dylan watched with growing appreciation as Meadow located the two wires running from the battery behind the seat and yanked. Once free it was an easy matter to touch the exposed ends together. The engine turned over.

"You ever drive one?" asked Meadow.

He shook his head and she climbed into the driver's seat.

"Where'd you learn that trick?" he asked.

"It's why I got thrown out of the Canton-Wesley Academy. Stole the dean's cart and drove it into the outdoor pool on a dare."

Dylan returned to the entrance to the garage and hit the button to open the automatic door. Outside the lifting door was a white Range Rover, and beside the vehicle stood Meadow's father, holding a pistol.

"Get in," he ordered.

"DADDY?" MEADOW SLID from the seat of the cart and stood on unsteady legs.

Dylan dragged a golf club from the closest bag, a wood, with a nice solid-looking head.

"What are you doing here?" she asked.

"No time. Let's go." Theron Wrangler looked behind him, down the road as if expecting company. He was sweating and pale, and he held his left hand across his middle as if he had suffered some injury.

This made no sense. He'd brought them here and now he wanted to move them. Dylan tried to puzzle out a reason and a possibility flickered in his mind. He slipped the club behind his back as Wrangler turned his pistol in Dylan's direction.

"You, too. Come on." He stepped back, giving them room to exit. "Who else is here?"

Meadow shook her head. "Your men already left."

"My men?"

"Joe Rhodes and Mark Perkinson. They said you paid them to leave us here. Why, Daddy?"

"No time now."

If Dylan didn't know better, he would think he was looking at a man who was truly frightened.

Dylan wondered at the choice of words, which made it seem as if Theron's life was also at risk, though he was the one pointing the gun.

The blast of a car horn was unmistakable. Through the smoke that swirled about the house, Dylan saw the white Mercedes sedan draw into the driveway, boxing in Wrangler's Range Rover. The rear door swung open and Dylan saw Lupe Wrangler, dressed in charcoal-gray slacks and a tailored orange blouse, lean from the compartment and motion wildly to her daughter, shouting to be heard above the approaching maelstrom.

"Niña, hurry."

Her father swung the pistol to aim at his wife. She lifted her hand as her eyes widened. A moment later her face went scarlet with rage.

"Don't go, Meadow. She's the one who drugged you," said her father.

Meadow looked from one parent to the next as confusion knit her brow.

What had Carter told Dylan, the name that his new wife had overheard…? *Wrangler*. Not Theron Wrangler. Just Wrangler. Could it have been Lupe Wrangler all along?

Meadow took a step toward her mother. Dylan grabbed her arm. She stared up at him. He shook his head.

"I think your father is telling the truth."

"What?" she asked.

Because poison was a woman's weapon, he thought. And because he'd never seen a mother so hostile toward a child, and because Meadow did not resemble her siblings, who all favored their mother. And because Lupe had the money and the legacy of environmental ruin. The pieces of the puzzle snapped into place. Daddy's little girl and the reason Meadow could never please her mother.

"Come on Meadow," called Lupe. "Right now. He won't shoot you."

Theron kept the gun aimed at his wife.

Meadow inched closer to Dylan, the only one she seemed to trust at the moment.

"Mama, did you drug me?" she asked.

"Don't call me that. Not ever again."

Meadow recoiled as if shot. Dylan wrapped an arm about her as she leaned heavily against him.

"Your father brought you home after his little chippie died. Said he'd be a good boy and help the cause if I just took you in as my own. Ha. Easier said than done."

"You're not my mother."

"Ding-ding." Lupe's voice chimed like the bells on a carnival midway.

Why hadn't Katrina ever told her? She must have known. They all must have known.

"You hate me," said Meadow.

Lupe rolled her eyes in disgust. "Drama. Always drama." Lupe said something into the vehicle's open door. Theron headed for cover, making it behind the stucco wall inside the garage as two men holding pistols left the sedan in unison. They stood flanking the sedan, using the doors for cover. Dylan dragged Meadow behind the golf cart.

Lupe's orders were clear. "Kill her and the Indian. Get my husband. Don't kill him."

Meadow gasped. "It's her. She did all this."

From his position, Dylan could see Theron waiting beside the open bay door.

"She's the head of BEAR," said Dylan.

Wrangler cast him a glance, his jaw set tight as he nodded. He was caught between his daughter and his wife.

"She took the explosives?"

Theron kept his focus on the approaching gunmen but answered. "Yes."

"Why?"

"She wants to restore the river."

"Which river?"

"Shut up, Theron," said Lupe.

"Your river," said Theron.

"Ruined with their hydroelectric plants and man-made reservoirs," said Lupe. "Dammed and filled with speedboats on lakes that never should have existed in the first place. It's a crime against the earth. Man doesn't own that river."

Lupe stepped into the garage and faced her husband.

"Give me the gun, Theron."

He didn't. Instead, he moved to open ground, standing between his daughter and his wife.

"You can't shoot them," said Theron. "The coroner will see the bullet hole."

"Not if you're burned badly enough."

"They'll see it, Lupe. Even your connections won't stop them from an autopsy."

She gave a half shrug. "They've served me well thus far."

Lupe was used to playing God, thought Dylan.

"If you don't put down that gun, I'll leave you here with them," she said.

Theron now faced the two armed men both with weapons aimed at him.

Without warning, he shot one of the two men in the chest. The wounded man fell as the second man fired. Theron spun.

"Don't shoot him," yelled Lupe.

Theron fell to one knee, the gun now trapped between his open hand and the garage floor.

"Get his gun, Joe," ordered Lupe.

Dylan waited until the remaining gunman stooped in front of Theron to retrieve the pistol. Then Dylan stood and threw his club. It flew end over end and hit the second gunman. Joe managed to get an arm up to shield himself from the worst of it. Dylan rushed him, lifting a putter from the bag as he charged forward. He'd practiced with a war club for many years, and he'd learned hand-to-hand combat in the US Marines. And he knew that he had a chance to break the shooter's arm before he redirected his aim from the floor. It all depended on how fast his opponent could move and how well he could aim.

Dylan swung the club with all his might.

Chapter Twenty

The blow connected with the raised arm at the same instant Dylan saw the flash from the barrel. There was a burning pain at his neck. The shooter's arm went slack as both bones in his forearm bent as if on an invisible hinge. The gun clattered to the floor and Lupe scrambled to retrieve it as Dylan's forward momentum took him into his opponent. Dylan straddled his attacker and Joe screamed in agony as he attempted to splint the broken bones by cradling his injured arm.

Dylan spun in an effort to recover the pistol, but Meadow already held the weapon.

"Theron!" shouted Lupe.

Lupe fell to her knees beside her husband as Meadow's father sprawled to the cement floor clutching his side.

"You idiot!" Lupe wailed. "Stay with me."

Lupe fell across her husband's chest as blood welled bright red from a wound on the left side of Theron's abdomen.

She lifted her bloodshot eyes to Meadow. "You killed him. With worry and now with this. I should have drowned you in the bathtub when you were a baby." She looked back to her husband whose breathing was coming in short pants. Clearly he was not dead. "But I didn't want to hurt him. He's my only weakness. My compass." She glared back at the child of her husband's infidelity. "And you stole him. Part of him was always yours. I hate you for that."

The hot wind now howled past the building. Dylan knew the sound, like a locomotive. The fire had reached them.

"Meadow, we have to go," he called.

Meadow dropped to her knees opposite her mother. Dylan could see her father's chest heaving in a labored, an unnatural rise and fall as his color went from pink to a ghostly gray. Dylan had seen that before, after an IED had taken out the Humvee in front of his, killing all the passengers. Her father was dying.

Dylan left his combatant writhing on the floor and went to Meadow, who had forgotten the gun in her hand, which now rested on her father's still chest.

"Daddy!" she shrieked.

Lupe reached for the gun that lay in her husband's cupped hand. Dylan kicked it clear. The weapon skittered across the floor and under the cart beside them.

Dylan took the pistol from Meadow's hand and lifted her to her feet. He kept the weapon raised and on Lupe as he checked for a pulse at Theron's throat and found none.

"He's gone, Meadow." He shouted to be heard above the shrieking wind.

She screamed and tried to drop back to her knees beside her father, but he pulled her away. Lupe's black eyes remained fixed on his.

"Come with us if you want to live," he said.

Lupe shook her head and draped herself over her husband.

"Mama. Come," cried Meadow.

Lupe closed her eyes against the sight of the child she had tolerated and raised on a diet of bile and neglect. Dylan pulled her to the Mercedes. The flames now rose up behind the house, taking the trees below the roofline and sending black smoke swirling into the sky.

Dylan pushed Meadow into the passenger seat. As he reached the driver's side, he saw the one Lupe had called Joe carrying the struggling Lupe over his shoulder. His other arm hung limp at his side.

He jumped over his fallen comrade as he ran toward Theron's white SUV.

Dylan reached the road as Joe got Lupe into her husband's abandoned Range Rover. He did not know if they had a weapon but preferred not having them behind him, so he reversed the sedan far back on the road as the Range Rover roared backward out of the drive.

"They left him," she cried, looking back at the open garage and the black smoke that made it impossible to see the two fallen men within.

Dylan jerked the shift into gear and hit the gas.

"He's gone, Meadow. I'm sorry."

She covered her hands and wept while Dylan faced the problem before him. The inferno was racing up the hillside and the only escape through the fire.

The houses on the winding road below their original position were already engulfed in flames, the telephone poles burning as flames spiraled upward to the sky. The trunks of the trees burned orange, sending plumes of fire into a scarlet sky.

"Put on your belt, Meadow," he said.

Ash and burning embers now rained down upon the hood of the sedan, reflecting orange and red as they skittered from the metallic surface to fall to the road.

"I can't see through the smoke," she said, clicking her belt across her middle.

Dylan knew the roads to this development because he had driven through them on the way to his appointment with Cheney. That clear day, under bright blue skies, he had seen the houses tucked into the rolling pine-covered hillside. All roads led down to the main highway. And that was why, at every intersection, he headed down. He didn't know how far up they had been transported or where the fire had jumped the road. But he did know that the highway was below them and that it was the only way out.

Meadow coughed and pointed away from the thick smoke blocking his view.

"That way," she said, choosing the clear road that led away from the fire.

"I spoke to Ray last night before the party. He said they were letting Pine View Springs go."

"But all these homes."

Built in a tinderbox of dry forest that had not had a fire in decades. The ground cover alone had enough fuel to take the development. Add the piñon pines and it was impossible. The very thing that drew them to this place, the green trees and mountain views, was what made the landscape so deadly. And her mother had tossed the match that started it all.

"Have to get to the highway," he said.

He wondered if her mother's driver had headed into the fire or away?

The visibility dropped to zero as he steered to where the road should be. The smoke lifted in time for him to see the fire at the shoulder sending yellow flames slithering across the asphalt like some living creature. He accelerated across the stream of fire, praying it did not ignite their gas tank and that the thick black smoke beyond came from a fire beside and not on the highway.

The smoke was so thick it no longer looked like day but some eerie combination of twilight and hell. He flicked off the lights because the beams were reflecting back against the gray smoke. They shot through the fire wall and into a blazing inferno to their right. A car sat before them fully engulfed in flames. Dylan veered around.

The blaze beside them was not orange. This was white with pink flames bursting skyward. He had seen this and it was very bad.

"My God," said Meadow.

This was the burn-over. The fire sweeping from one side of the road to the other, flying on the winds of its own making. Fire and burning debris whisked from one side to the other. Dylan wondered if his decision to make for the highway had been a mistake. It seemed already too late.

He glanced to Meadow and felt a strangled hope mixed with bitter regret. He could see a life with her if they could escape the flames but he could also see their chances of escape burning to ash.

"I'm sorry," he said.

She lowered her chin as the significance of his words reached her. She did not look frightened or torn with sorrow. She looked pissed.

"Don't you give up on us. We are getting out of this."

Dylan nodded and pushed the sedan to greater speeds. He couldn't see the road at times, but he could see the blackened earth on either side of them.

"It's been past here," she called, her voice elated. "The fire."

Meadow was a fast learner. She understood what that meant.

Nothing left to burn. Not the shells of two-by-fours that had once been luxury housing or the smoldering trunks of denuded trees that had once been green with pine needles or the blackened smoldering frames of automobiles stripped of rubber and glass by the raging wildfire.

They had reached a burn-over.

"Keep going. The highway can't be far."

She was right. The smoke now hung above them like the anvil head of a huge electrical storm. But the road before them was clear. Dylan allowed himself to exhale.

"Do you think they got through?" Meadow asked.

Her mother. The woman who had drugged her and dropped her in the path of a wildfire—twice.

"Meadow," he said.

"I know." She cradled her head in her hands. "She hated me. Now I understand why."

Dylan exhaled slowly, trying to unravel the tangle of emotions that came with family. Her mother despised her. But Meadow couldn't do the same. No matter how awful, that was her mother—or the only mother she had ever known. Perhaps with her father's death, she might never find the name of her real one.

"I'm sorry, Meadow. And, yes, they might have gotten through." If they had come down the hillside, he thought.

Ahead, Dylan spotted flashing blue lights and slowed as the emergency vehicles came into view. The roadblock was staffed by a female officer, who wore a yellow vest over her uniform and waved a flashlight to help him see her. Dylan slowed and rolled down his window.

"You both all right?" she asked, bending to speak to Dylan. "Mister, you're bleeding."

Dylan touched the wound at his neck, feeling the clotting blood in the gash carved through skin and muscle by the bullet.

"I'm all right. Anyone else come this way recently?"

She shook her head, still staring at his neck.

"That looks bad."

"I'm on my way to medical now. Can you radio the FBI?"

"FBI? Why?"

"There are two people still up there. One is wanted. The other shot me."

"You two better pull over."

Dylan did and answered her questions while accepting some gauze from her medical kit. She let him use her mobile and he got through to Forrest, flipping the call to speaker and then explaining their situation.

"She's up there?" asked Forrest.

"I think so. Only one way out and we're at it."

"So she still might get out?"

"Possibly."

"Tell the officer not to stop them but to notify me if that Range Rover passes her position. I've got people en route. You two head for Flagstaff and our offices there."

Meadow shook her head and spoke up. "Hospital. He's been shot in the neck and there's a gash on the back of his head."

"You better drive, Meadow," said Forrest. "I'm sending help. They'll meet you."

Dylan returned the phone to the officer who did not detain them.

They switched seats. Meadow drove them toward help and they were intercepted twenty miles outside of the city by an ambulance. Dylan's headache had only gotten worse and the smoke and the blood loss made him woozy and sick to his stomach. He needed help to stand and to get onto the gurney. Meadow abandoned the sedan to ride with him to the hospital. He didn't remember much of it, just the IV going in.

Meadow sat beside him, her face smudged with ash and soot. But they had made it out. Dylan closed his eyes and let himself drift. But drifting was dangerous. You never knew which way the current would take you.

He heard Meadow calling him back, but he just couldn't summon the strength.

AT THE FLAGSTAFF HOSPITAL, they took Dylan through a double door and into Emergency, where she could not follow. She called Jack and told him what had happened. He said they would send his family and tribal leadership.

She was treated and released to the custody of the FBI. Neither Field Agent Forrest nor Field Agent Cassidy Cosen arrived to interview her. Instead she was grilled by Special Agent Virginia Bicher. It became apparent quickly that she did not believe one word Meadow said.

"I want a lawyer," she said.

"You're not under arrest, Miss Wrangler. We're just investigating a crime you allege was committed."

"Did you find my mother?"

"Let me ask the questions, please."

After that Meadow closed her mouth. Following another barrage of questions she would not answer, she stood up to leave.

"We're not finished yet," said Agent Bicher.

"I'm finished." Meadow walked out, expecting to be arrested or detained. But they let her go. She still wore her silver satin dress, now torn, soot covered and smelling of smoke. She had no shoes and her stockings had run at both knees. It was this picture that was captured by the news media waiting outside FBI headquarters. Meadow was forced to return to the lobby. Then she faced a dilemma. She had no money. No credit cards. She called her sister Katrina for help.

Katrina came in a limo ninety minutes later, having driven up from Phoenix with a driver and a bodyguard, who plowed a path through the reporters and herded Meadow into the backseat where her sister was waiting.

"What did you do now?" Katrina said by way of a greeting. "Mom is furious. She could barely speak to me."

"Mom's alive?"

"What?"

"You talked to Mom?" Meadow felt she had dropped down the rabbit hole again. "When?"

"She said you called Dad out of bed last night and you two took off to film the fire." Katrina waved a hand before her face. "God, you reek."

The bodyguard climbed into the passenger seat and glanced back at Katrina. She nodded.

"Go," she said, and then touched the button to lift the privacy shield between them and the men seated in front of them.

The limo pulled away from the throng of photographers still snapping photos.

"Why did you go back up there?" asked Katrina.

Meadow shook her head in denial. "I didn't. I was drugged."

"You mean you drank too much."

"I had two glasses of wine."

"More like six. I was there, remember."

Meadow's skin began to crawl. "Take me to the hospital."

"More reporters there. Mom said to bring you home. She actually said to leave you, but I talked her out of that. You can thank me later."

"Katrina, Mom had me kidnapped and she tried to have me killed."

Katrina gave Meadow a long, steady stare. With that frown, her older sister looked exactly like their mom. Meadow corrected herself. Lupe Wrangler was not her mother and that explained so very much, because no matter how good or bad she was, Meadow had never managed to earn more than Lupe Wrangler's disdain.

Her sister lifted one of Meadow's eyelids. "Are you high?"

Meadow pulled away. "No." She captured her sister's hand. "You have to take me to your apartment. I can't see Mom."

"You have to face her sometime."

"But you spoke to her. Really?"

"You are acting so odd."

"What time is it?" asked Meadow, glancing at the dashboard clock.

"Three. Why?"

"Saturday?"

"Yes, of course."

Katrina's phone jangled a tune and she glanced down.

"It's Phillip." She lay an elegant, manicured finger over the screen and then lifted the smartphone. "Hi, Phil. What's up?" Katrina listened. "Yes. I have her. Reporters everywhere." A pause. "I didn't know about the press until I got there." Another pause as her eyebrows lifted. "I'm putting you on speaker. You can ask her." Katrina switched the call to speaker. "Go ahead."

Phillip's voice emerged. "Meadow? Dad's missing. Mom said he left with you in the Range Rover last night. Do you know where he is?"

Meadow blurted out her story, choking on tears.

"Wait. Wait," Phillip said. "Start from the beginning. You left with Dad late last night, and you two drove into the neighborhood that had been evacuated. Then what happened?"

"That's *not* what happened. I was kidnapped from my room."

"I saw you leave with him, Meadow."

"I was taken by Joe Rhodes and Mark Perkinson."

"Who?"

"Joe. Dad's sound guy."

"I don't know him, Meadow. What was the other name?"

"Mark Perkinson. He's Rosalie's legal assistant."

"Her legal assistant is Jessica Navade. I know because I approve all hires. I'll check with HR, but I don't know anyone named Perkinson."

"That's impossible. I've met them. You've met them."

"Katrina? Take me off speaker."

Her sister instantly complied.

"Yes. Mmm-hmm. I agree. Okay. Will do."

Meadow's mind spun as she tried to make sense of what was happening.

"Where was Mom last night?" asked Meadow.

"At your party."

"Today, I mean."

"Rosalie said they had breakfast and then Mom left to see Phillip about the gala."

"Phillip said she was with him?"

There was no disguising the impatience as Katrina hissed out a yes. "Why?"

"Someone is lying. She wasn't there."

Katrina sat back in her seat and gave Meadow a look of displeasure.

"So Phillip's lying and Rosalie is lying? Everyone. Right?"

Meadow stared at her sister. Either Katrina really didn't know what was happening or she was a part of this. Suddenly Meadow felt as if she was back in that fire shelter struggling to breathe. What was happening?

Chapter Twenty-One

Meadow inched closer to the door as her older sister huffed out a breath. Katrina sank back in the plush leather seat and folded her arms as she tapped out her impatience with her index finger on her sleeve. She stared at the ceiling as she spoke, her voice laden with reproach.

"Of all the attention-getting stunts you have pulled, this takes the cake." She rolled her head on the headrest to stare at Meadow. "What's wrong with you?"

"Me? Katrina, have you seen Dad? He's gone."

"What did you do to him?"

Meadow faced the obvious truth. Either her mother had played Phillip and Katrina, or they were fully informed and this was some kind of mass cover-up. Well, they couldn't hide two bodies or her father's absence. But they could pin both on her. She sucked in a breath as she realized they might also pin the murders on Dylan.

"I have to make a phone call," said Meadow, reaching for Katrina's phone.

Her sister held it back. "Not yet." Katrina lowered the privacy shield between the front and rear seating area and passed her phone to the bodyguard. Then she spoke to her driver.

"Change of plans, Ralph. Could you take us to this address?"

The driver glanced down and his eyebrows lifted. "Yes ma'am."

"Where? Where are you taking me?" said Meadow, her voice taking on a hysterical edge.

"Take it easy, Meadow."

"I want out of this car. Right now!"

Katrina rolled her eyes. "So dramatic." Then she spoke to Ralph. "Hurry, would you?"

"Yes, ma'am."

The car sped on and Katrina lifted the privacy shield. "You're embarrassing me."

Meadow tried to explain again, from the beginning. Katrina rolled her eyes up and away and folded her arms.

"Where are we going?"

"To a hospital."

Meadow sat back as dread slithered in her belly, cold and slippery as an eel. "What kind of hospital?"

"FMHH."

She gasped. She'd spent time at Flagstaff Mental Health Hospital before, when she was just seventeen. Her mother had taken her for a drug test that had come back positive for opiates and she'd been admitted. She'd learned that going in was a lot easier than getting out, especially for a teen. She'd spent three months there.

"You need my permission."

Katrina shrugged. "Phillip says you need help. I agree. We think you're drinking again."

"I'm not!"

"You had wine last night."

"So did you," said Meadow.

"I'm not an alcoholic."

"This is Mother's idea, isn't it?"

Katrina didn't deny it. "She's worried about you. And Dad's missing. Now you're making up stories and people. You never made up people before."

"I'm not making this up. Katrina, you have to believe me."

Her sister just shook her head. "You'll be all over the newspapers again. A media frenzy. Congratulations. You'll be in the tabloids all week. Front page. Just look at yourself." She swept a hand toward Meadow. "Who goes to a forest fire in a satin cocktail dress? Oh, my baby sister, that's who."

They left the highway and Meadow considered her options. They couldn't admit her if she refused treatment. She was an adult, after all. She didn't think diving out of a moving car would improve her chances of looking sane. She would need to convince the doctors to contact the FBI and tribal police.

"But what if Mother had gotten to them, too?" she muttered.

"Gotten to whom? A hospital? Meadow, you sound crazy. You know that, right?"

At the hospital admissions, she was muscled into an exam room by two goons. Once in an exam room, it was explained to her that they did not need her permission for an evaluation because three of her family members had requested one.

She was told that she was being admitted because her family believed her likely to suffer mental or physical harm due to impaired judgment and that she had displayed symptoms of substance abuse.

Meadow refused evaluation and was told that her inability to appreciate the need for such services only strengthened the argument for involuntary placement. Her best option was to cooperate.

Then the intake physician showed her a petition for involuntary emergency admission signed by her mother, Phillip and Katrina. It was in that moment, as she held the page between her two trembling hands, that Meadow recognized that even if she explained the truth she would sound paranoid and, well, crazy.

Once admitted—she had no doubt that the evaluation would recommend admission—she would be either locked away here or killed in some accidental fashion. A suicide, perhaps. Her family had done an excellent job in discrediting her. What police detective, FBI agent or jury would believe a woman twice institutionalized?

It was in that moment of betrayal by her family that her mind turned from convincing others of her sanity to plans of escape.

THE SUNLIGHT FROM the window hurt Dylan's eyes even through his closed lids. Gradually he realized the sounds around him were unfamiliar and there was something wrong with his neck. The dull ache at his elbow caused him to bend the joint, sending off an alarm beeping beside him.

"You awake?"

Someone straightened his arm and the beeping stopped.

He knew the voice. That was Jack Bear Den.

Dylan cracked open an eye and stared. He tried to speak and the movement caused his neck to throb.

"What?" asked Jack. "Don't talk yet. Just listen."

Jack sat in the chair beside his bed. Two more people sat behind him on a bench beneath the window. The railing between him and Jack confirmed his suspicion. He was lying in a hospital bed.

"You were shot in the throat. Lost a lot of blood from that neck wound. The bullet grazed muscle mostly but nicked the artery. You're lucky, Brother Bobcat. Very lucky."

Dylan tapped his wrist and then raised the wrist to his ear.

"Time? It's still Sunday. Seven p.m. You came in by ambulance yesterday morning and went right in to surgery. After that they kept you in the ICU overnight because of your blood pressure."

"What was wrong with my blood pressure?" he whispered.

"You didn't have one."

Dylan lifted a hand to touch the bandage at his neck. His voice had sounded strange. The pain told him that something was wrong with his throat.

THE TWO PEOPLE at the window rose and approached him. As soon as they moved past the flood of late-afternoon sunlight through the open blinds, he recognized his mother, Dotty, and his maternal grandfather, Frank Florez.

His mother took his hand and began to cry. His grandfather rested a gnarled hand on Dylan's thigh and forced a smile.

"Welcome back, grandson," he said in Tonto Apache.

"Where's...?" His voice rasped like sandpaper across stone.

"They stitched up your neck. A gash. The rest is bumps and bruises."

Dylan pressed a hand to his throat, feeling the thick bandage, and then moved his fingers to rub over his Adam's apple and winced.

"They had to open your airway in the ER to get more oxygen into your blood. They stuck a tube down your throat. Oh, and you had some transfusions."

"Meadow?" he whispered.

Jack bowed his head. "Can't find her."

"What?" He tried to get up, and both his friend and grandfather pushed him back down. The fact that he was so easily subdued scared him almost as much as learning that Meadow was missing.

"I've got Forrest looking. She was with you here. The ER nurse I spoke to said she tried to get to you. But she wasn't family so...she was treated for minor injuries and released. The FBI questioned her. Dylan, where's Theron Wrangler?"

"Shot," he said.

Jack winced. "That's what Forrest said, and that Meadow told one of their investigators, Field Agent Bicher, the same. They've been out searching for evidence to confirm her story, but the fire has made it impossible to reach some places. Meadow didn't know where exactly you two were. Do you know?"

"Pine View somewhere." He winced at the pain words caused him but it didn't stop him. "Her mother?"

"Here. Here all the time, according to her statement. She's got witnesses."

"No," he whispered. "Lying. Her man. Shot me."

"Could Theron Wrangler have been the one who shot you?"

"What? No." Dylan held a hand to his throbbing neck and clamped the other around Jack's wrist. "Find her."

"Working on it. Family asked for privacy."

"They have her? They'll kill her," rasped Dylan. "Call Forrest."

"I did. He's investigating Meadow's story. So far he hasn't found a shred of evidence that any of this happened. He has no bodies and no crime scene."

Dylan pointed to the bullet wound. "He has this."

"I'll call him again. Already left four messages."

Dylan threw back the white sheet and thin cotton blanket.

"What are you doing?" asked Jack.

"I'm going to find Meadow."

"No, you're not."

Dylan was going. Jack wasn't stopping him. Dylan did not wait for the discharge papers, but he was delayed while his mother went to buy him some jeans and a shirt because they'd cut off his clothing in the ER. Luckily, his boots and turquoise necklace had both survived. Once she returned, he dressed and slipped the multistrand of turquoise over his head before he tugging on his boots.

"Your neck is bleeding," said Jack, raising a finger to point at the bandage.

Dylan flashed an impatient glance from Jack to his mother, who stood at the foot of his bed with a newspaper clutched to her chest. Dylan paused. Her mother never bought the newspaper, preferring to get her news from Native Peoples Television and NPR. This particular one had the distinctive shape of the tabloid news.

"Mom?" Dylan rasped.

"She's in the paper." Dotty slowly lowered the paper so that he could see the headline and photo beneath—Meadow Burnin' Down the Houz!

Beneath was Meadow still in her tattered soot-smeared party dress, lifting a hand to shield her face from the flashes of the paparazzi's camera.

Dylan scanned the article. Meadow had been photographed leaving the FBI office in Flagstaff yesterday afternoon with two "handlers," who looked like gorillas in suits.

He read aloud. "No comment from family." He lifted his head. "She's disappeared. The reporters were waiting at her parents' home. She never showed." He flipped the page, read the continuing article. Then his hands dropped and the paper crumpled in his lap.

"What?"

"Unidentified source claims she checked into rehab."

Jack snatched the paper. "Where?"

Dylan shook his head. "We have to get her."

"Hold on. Let me get my hat," said Jack.

Jack's phone rang and he drew it from his front pocket. "It's Forrest."

Jack answered the phone and kept his eyes on Dylan.

"Yeah."

Dylan could hear Luke speaking, but the words were unclear.

"Okay." Jack disconnected. "We gotta get out of here. Now."

Dylan had been ready to leave, but now he hesitated. "Why?"

"Forrest is on his way. They found two bodies up in Pine View. He has orders to bring you in for questioning."

Chapter Twenty-Two

"Why did Forrest call us first?" asked Dylan as they reached the parking lot and Jack's tribal police unit, a large white SUV with blue lettering on the sides.

"I'd say to give us a head start," said Jack, opening the passenger door.

Dylan was about to object to being driven around, but it hurt to talk, and even climbing up into the seat made him sweat.

"He told me that agents interviewed Lupe Wrangler. She was seen retiring last night a little after eleven and her staff confirmed she ate breakfast at six at her home. She provided access to her cook and housekeeper and driver. All corroborated her version of events."

"Lying," said Dylan, and he winced.

"Well, then so is her family. She met with one of her daughters in the morning and the caterers for a gala that PAN is having in the fall. She's got a solid alibi."

Dylan shook his head. It didn't happen that way. He had seen her. But when? Early Saturday morning in the hours before she had breakfast? He didn't know what time he'd woken on that patio beside Meadow.

The smoke had been so thick it might have been morning or night.

"How'd she get from the fire to Flagstaff?" asked Jack. "She never passed the roadblock."

"Helicopter? Meadow's father picked us up outside the rez in one." Dylan had to hold his throat against the pain and felt the blood soaking through the bandages.

"Maybe. I'll ask Forrest to do some checking. She can't cover flight records."

"Want to bet?" asked Dylan. He climbed into the passenger side and buckled up, waiting with impatience for Jack to get them moving. Then he realized he didn't know where to start.

"Any ideas?" asked Jack.

Dylan bowed his head to think. Who would know something and be willing to tell them?

"She told me Katrina looked out for her when they were kids."

"Where does she live?"

"I don't know."

Jack started typing on his computer. In a few minutes the database search provided Katrina's vehicle registration, violations, and property.

"Katrina likes to drive too fast," said Jack.

Dylan leaned in and found her residential address. "Let's go."

The drive to Phoenix seemed endless. Finally they pulled up before the complex. Katrina's posh apartment was located on the top floor. Jack's badge got them access, but Katrina knew they were coming.

She met them at her door and escorted them to her

living room, glancing several times over her shoulder toward the kitchen.

"Who else is here?" asked Jack.

"My housekeeper," said Katrina. "My mother picked her."

The implication was clear. Katrina was worried her mother would find out she was speaking to the enemy.

She swept them past her housekeeper and told the young woman that she was not to be disturbed. Once inside, she shut the door and pressed her back against it as if to bar the castle gates.

Dylan glanced about the room, seeing a white leather couch edged in chrome opposite a glass coffee table from two matching chairs. The banks of windows provided impressive views and were anchored with a long, curving cabinets in ivory, which hugged the bend in the exterior wall. Her glass-and-chrome fireplace dominated the room. The only color was a cheerful bouquet that sat on the coffee table beside her television remotes.

"What are you two doing here?" She spoke in a whisper that held a definite edge.

"Where is she?" asked Dylan.

She lifted a finger. "You're bleeding." She stared at his neck and spoke as if to herself. "I should call security."

"She said you looked out for her," Dylan said.

Katrina sucked in a breath and her chin trembled.

Dylan bowed his head and spoke in a calm, gentle voice. "She needs you now more than ever."

Katrina folded her arms around herself and began

to rock, thumping back against the closed door. Finally she shook her head. "You should go."

He wasn't going. Not until he knew where to find her. "Katrina, they're going to kill her."

"You're as crazy as she is."

"If you're right, it won't matter. But what if I'm right?"

Katrina stopped rocking and glared. He waited, knowing that the one to speak first in this standoff would lose.

"She's at Flagstaff Mental Health Hospital," said Katrina, her voice low and conspiratorial. "They're holding her for observation and I never told you. Now get out."

"A psychiatric hospital?" asked Jack.

"She asked me to bring her."

"Your mother?" asked Jack.

Katrina nodded.

"Because Meadow trusted you," said Dylan.

Katrina flinched, then lifted her chin in an attitude of defiance. "They found barbiturates in her blood."

Dylan paused. "Want to know who put them there?"

Katrina turned her worried eyes away. "You should go."

Dylan was already heading for the door and Katrina swept out of the way. "You won't get her out. It's very secure."

Dylan didn't know how he'd get to her, but he knew one thing for sure—he would get to Meadow.

Jack followed him out. Once back in the tribal police unit, Jack hit the lights and then the highway, driving at high speeds and using the siren to move distracted drivers out of their way.

Dylan turned to his friend.

"We need to break her out."

"You have a plan?" Jack asked. "Because I have zero jurisdiction and no friends down here. I might as well pull up on a Segway dressed as a mall cop."

"Steal someone's ID card?"

"Illegal."

Dylan swore. "Every plan I come up with will be illegal." He wondered what they were doing to her right now. "They could stage a suicide attempt."

"Not if she's under observation. She'd be under added supervision and it will be harder for anyone to hurt her."

Dylan hoped Jack was right.

Dylan felt his stomach drop. "Drive faster," he said.

Jack pressed the accelerator slowing only when they reached their exit. He took them to the facility, which had a high metal gate and security booth at the entrance.

"That's bad," said Jack.

"Obviously." Dylan scratched his head and found the smooth surface of the staples they had used to close up his scalp. "What about a laundry service or food service truck?"

"Still check ID and we wouldn't have access past the delivery area. What you need is someone who can go anywhere, even to the lock-in floors."

"Impersonate a doctor?"

Jack gave a halfhearted shrug.

Dylan's throat hurt. His head hurt. But, most of

all, his heart hurt. Meadow was in there alone, and he had to get to her before her mother finished what she had started.

Someone who could go anywhere, he thought, and then the idea came to him, all at once and completely formed.

"That might work," Dylan muttered.

"What?" asked Jack.

"Fire inspector," said Dylan.

"I don't follow," said Jack Bear Den, still staring at the front gate to the mental-health facility.

"I'm a certified fire inspector."

"On Turquoise Canyon," said Jack.

"No. Statewide. I can inspect any public facility, including group homes, residential-care facilities and medical facilities."

"But not at night," said Jack.

"Oh, yeah. Especially at night. If they do business in the evening, like a bar, or 24/7, like a hospital, I can inspect them anytime, any day."

Jack sat back and smiled. "Ain't that a kick?"

"They're inspected quarterly and they are not supposed to know ahead of time."

"What if they just got inspected yesterday?" Jack asked.

"Doesn't matter. I tell them that there has been a complaint of a code violation."

"You have a badge or something?" asked Jack.

"I do, but not with me. But I have an ID card in my wallet. Two, actually—state and international."

"My vehicle says Tribal Police," said Jack.

"Yeah, we need to lose this. Where's Ray?"

"He's back on the line, fighting the fire. They're making progress now. He says it's seventy percent contained. We could rent a vehicle."

"A red or white SUV."

"City vehicle would be better," said Jack. He threw the SUV into Reverse. "Shouldn't be very hard to find one to borrow at this time of night."

"Sounds like a plan."

"Once we find her, how do we get her out?" asked Jack.

"I might need your help on that one."

Dylan used Jack's phone to find city hall. Round the back on West Aspen Avenue was a really nice parking lot with a variety of white vehicles all with the city's colorful insignia on the door panel. They had vans and midsize cars, SUVs and several pickups. Dylan walked along with Jack as he selected a pickup that was shielded from the street by three other cars.

"They'll have cameras on this lot," said Jack.

Which was why they had left the tribal police car down the street and walked here with Jack's bag of tools. His friend routinely broke into cars for various reasons.

Dylan glanced about as Jack used the slim jim to pop the door open. He wedged his big shoulders between the seat and wheel well and had the truck started soon after. Dylan drove the truck, pausing only to drop Jack at his vehicle before retracing his course back to the facility holding Meadow.

He felt the pressure of time pushing down on him. Was her mother's plan merely to discredit Meadow or did she mean to kill her?

Jack flashed his lights and then passed him as he turned into the residential neighborhood close to the hospital. He parked on the street and then joined Dylan.

"Okay, let's go."

At the gate they found a sleepy attendant who snapped into action as Dylan identified himself and presented his ID.

"Usually we know ahead," said the pink-faced attendant as he studied the red-and-white identification card.

"You're not supposed to have advance warning. Who's been doing the inspections?"

That got the young man twitching. He closed his mouth and scribbled down Dylan's name and ID number. Then he lifted the phone in the booth.

Jack leaned across the seat and yelled, "Gate!"

A moment later the lever arm lifted and they drove on.

He did and they rolled up to the facility. They had not even disconnected the starter wires when a woman came rushing out to meet them.

Chapter Twenty-Three

Meadow woke with the taste of copper in her mouth. Her head pounded and her vision rippled like moonlight reflecting on deep water. The cotton dressing gown stuck to her wet skin and sweat puddled beneath her flushed body. The movement of her eyes caused sharp pains at her temples. She hadn't felt like this since she'd stopped drinking Jack.

This was a hospital. She knew the look of the sterile walls and room layout. Meadow tried to lift her hand to scratch her nose and found her wrist secured to the bed rail with a clear plastic tie. Above the fastening was a white hospital bracelet.

The panic bubbled up inside her as the intake process rose in her mind like a backed-up toilet. She'd been stripped. She'd been searched. They'd taken her clothing, earrings, underwear, blood and, finally, her dignity. When she'd refused their tests they'd injected her with something.

Where was Dylan? Did he know what had happened to her? What if they had hurt him? The last she'd seen him was in the emergency room, where he was being treated for a bullet wound. Shot by her mother's crony.

Oh, the blood. So much blood.

Meadow squeezed her eyes shut. This was all her fault. She'd dragged him into this nightmare and he'd stayed and it had nearly gotten him killed.

She prayed he was alive and safe. But in the meantime she needed to get out of here.

"Hey," she yelled. "Hey! I need to use the toilet."

Someone stepped into her room. She knew him. Meadow gasped as the face of Joe Rhodes came into focus. He was dressed like a male nurse or orderly in green scrubs and white tennis shoes. His left arm was casted and now rested in a black sling. If Meadow found any solace, it was in knowing that Dylan had broken Joe's arm in the fight at the ridge fire.

"Good evening, Princess."

"Joe, whatever my mother is paying you, I'll double it."

He smiled. "She said you'd try to bribe me, so she cut off your funds. They're her funds. You don't have anything without her." He stepped nearer. "Oh, your blood work came back." He ticked the items off on the fingers of his injured arm. "Oxy. Barbiturates. Pot, of course. And heroin. Looks like you've moved up from binge drinking."

"You know she put all that in my drink."

"No, actually, I did. I had a tranquilizer in there, too, but it didn't come up on the test. Must have worked it out of your system."

He stepped nearer.

"I'll scream."

He grimaced. "Oh, please. Someone is screaming in here about every three minutes."

"Stay back." She used her legs to push as far away from him as her bonds allowed. Panic zinged through her like speed and her heart crashed into her ribs. She was going to die here in this stupid bed with the sheets tangled about her legs and everyone in the world would believe she was just another train wreck.

"You're on suicide watch," Joe said, now at her bedside. "I wrapped the IV tube around your neck, but someone came in before I finished. Got you restrained, though."

"How are you going to explain my killing myself while restrained?"

"Bit your tongue." He reached for her, grabbing her head and sealing her nose shut.

She struggled and finally had to open her mouth. He pushed a wedge of plastic between her jaws. Meadow was not ready to die. She rolled her knees to her chest and then exploded outward like a diver before entering the water. Only, instead of extending toward a perfect entry, she kicked Joe's casted arm with all her might.

Joe screamed and fell back, landing hard on the floor. Meadow spit out the wedge and shimmied down in her bed, gnawing at the restraint on her right wrist. Joe was on his feet and cradling his arm as she pulled one wrist free.

There was murder in his eyes as he approached her bed for the second time.

DYLAN ADDRESSED HIS attention to Louisa Crane, the night manager on call, who had drawn the short straw for taking the inspectors throughout the facility. She was dressed in a black skirt and maroon blouse, and her black hair was drawn back in a neat ponytail. She was young with anxious eyes.

"Let's start with the sprinkler systems," said Dylan to Louisa. He knew that the sprinklers were on every floor and every room. It was a way to get to Meadow quickly. But, when and if he found her, how would he get her out?

"Oh, all right," said Louisa.

"And the fire exits. You can't have equipment blocking stairways."

"Oh, we never do," said Crane, but she was sweating now, her dark blouse showing even darker stains down the center of her back.

She swiped her employee card in a slot to summon the elevator and again inside to access the top floor, level three.

"This is a lock-in ward with some of the residents who wander. It can be noisy."

"When was your last fire drill?" asked Dylan.

Crane wiped her upper lip. "I'd have to check the records. I'm only here at night."

"You have to run drills day and night. Practice is important," said Jack, sounding as if he knew what he was talking about.

Crane's hand went to the junction of her neck and shoulder where she rubbed. Dylan smiled. Apparently Jack and he were becoming a pain in her neck.

"I need to check the dates on the extinguishers and see the sprinkler heads in every room," said Dylan.

"Every room?" Crane did not keep the exasperation from her voice. "That will disturb the patients."

"I need to see eighteen inches of clearance under each sprinkler head."

He began his inspection in the room to his left and continued to the next and the next.

The crash brought them all around. A male voice roared and a woman shouted for help. Dylan glanced at Jack and nodded. He knew that voice. It was Meadow.

Dylan turned in the direction of the commotion and charged down the hall.

"Hey!" called Crane.

The sound of something striking metal reached him as he barreled into the room.

Jack followed Dylan and the two men skidded to a stop in front of the hospital bed and the two struggling combatants.

A man in a sling choked Meadow as she thrashed, her heel striking the bed rail and making it ring as she clawed at the hand clamped to her throat.

Crane arrived and gasped. "What is going on here?"

Her attacker released Meadow, but she continued to swing, her arms and legs flaying as she fought for her life. His brave warrior would not go down without a fight.

"Meadow," Dylan called.

At the sound of his voice, her eyes popped open and her body stilled.

Crane gaped. "You know her? What is this?"

The man now faced them. Dylan braced as he recognized Joe Rhodes.

Crane drew out her phone and started pressing buttons.

Dylan inched along the opposite side of the bed from Rhodes as Jack stepped past the foot of the bed to block Rhodes's exit.

Tears rolled down Meadow's face as she looked at Dylan.

"You…you came," said Meadow,

Had she doubted that he would?

Dylan reached for the small knife clipped to his belt and flipped open one of the blades.

"Weapons are not allowed in here," said Crane.

Dylan ignored her as he sliced the bond holding her left wrist to the bed rail.

"You can't do that," said Crane.

Meadow threw herself into Dylan's arms. He gathered her up and held her, whispering in her ear.

"I got you."

"I need your ID badge. Now," said Crane to Rhodes.

Rhodes spoke to no one in particular. "We've got company."

"He just called for backup," Jack said.

Rhodes reached into the sling. He drew a pistol at the same time Jack drew his sidearm from his shoulder holster. Rhodes pointed his weapon at Meadow, now on the opposite side of the bed, as Jack leveled his service pistol at Rhodes.

Crane closed her mouth and inched back toward the door.

Jack did not move. Dylan knew Jack was an excellent shot, but he was not fast enough to stop Joe from firing at Meadow.

Stalemate.

"I'll step aside and you can go," said Jack, who did not move aside but kept his weapon raised and ready.

"Lower your weapon," said Rhodes.

Jack didn't move. Dylan eased Meadow to the floor and then stepped in front of her.

Rhodes shifted his attention to Dylan. "Bullet will go right through you and then hit her. It won't even slow down."

Jack spoke again. "You should go."

Rhodes did not take his eyes off his targets. "Put the gun on the floor, Bear Den."

Dylan knew that Jack would not do so. If he did, there was nothing to keep Rhodes from shooting all of them.

Dylan spoke in Apache. "Shoot him."

Jack said nothing, just kept his weapon poised and ready. Rhodes was sweating now, the beads rolling down his face and into his eyes. He shrugged his shoulder, but with the cast he could not wipe his face.

Crane continued her backward tread until she inched from Dylan's view behind the wall and the corridor that led past the bathroom and into the main hallway. A moment later, Dylan heard a shot coming from the hallway. Rhodes's gaze shifted away from Meadow and toward the door.

Jack fired.

Chapter Twenty-Four

Rhodes crashed to the floor on the opposite side of the bed.

"Check him," said Jack as he moved toward the door. "Crane is down."

Dylan rounded the bed toward the motionless Rhodes, catching a glimpse of the woman's body sprawled in the hall outside Meadow's room and of Jack pressed to the wall beside the door, weapon raised.

Meadow followed Dylan as far as the foot of the bed.

"Get down," said Dylan, and Meadow crouched.

Dylan checked Rhodes and found no pulse. Jack had hit him in the breastbone. Dylan retrieved the man's pistol from the floor.

"Two heading this way," said Jack from the door. "Armed with rifles."

Dylan went to the window and glanced out at the night. Meadow's room sat directly over the entrance, three floors down, but there was a flat portico one story beneath them.

Dylan used the chair to smash the window and lowered Meadow over the window casements.

"Get ready," he said. She nodded, and he dropped her. She landed on her feet and then fell to her side. He turned to Jack. "You're next."

"What have we got?" said Jack, retreating backward toward Dylan's position.

"Portico on two, about ten feet down."

"Together, then," he said.

They went out the window, using the casements to dangle to full length before dropping beside Meadow.

Gunfire sounded above them.

"They're in the room," said Jack, raising his weapon and aiming at the windows above them.

Dylan helped Meadow to her feet. She was unsteady and pale as moonlight. What had they given her in there?

He helped her to the edge of the portico. Jack was already on the ground beside the entrance with his service pistol raised. He fired three shots as Dylan lifted Meadow and sent her over the edge once more.

The instant she landed, he dropped beside her, and all three made it under cover as the two gunman above returned fire.

"They'll be down as fast as they can take those stairs," said Jack.

"Let's go."

Dylan never let go of Meadow's hand as they raced along the sidewalk, close to the building and then out to the lot. Alarm bells sounded behind them. Their pursuers had reached ground level.

Jack opened the door to the city vehicle and Dylan

lifted Meadow inside before scrambling up beside her. When Jack reached the driver's seat, he touched the exposed wires together and the truck engine turned over. They pulled away and out of the gate, making the turn as the lights of the police units swarmed past them.

"Your neck is bleeding again," said Jack.

"We need to lose this car," said Dylan.

Meadow clung to Dylan, burying her face against the muscles of his chest. He rubbed her shoulder and held her tight.

"I've got you, Meadow. And I'm not letting go."

They switched vehicles at Jack's police unit near the Flagstaff lot and headed east toward their reservation, taking the winding route past the series of reservoirs until they reached Turquoise Canyon land. Meadow slept on his shoulder much of the way. Dylan kept one arm around her and the opposite hand pressed to his neck wound, which had come alive with a throbbing ache now that the adrenaline had ebbed away to nothing.

Jack called ahead and a welcoming committee waited at the tribe's health clinic. The group included Jack's brother Kurt, the paramedic, Kenshaw Little Falcon and Jack's boss, the chief of tribal police, Wallace Tinnin.

"You about to get fired?" asked Dylan, eyeing the sour expression on Tinnin's face.

"Or promoted. Hard to tell."

"Is that Forrest?" said Dylan, looking at the man standing beside tribal police chief Wallace Tinnin.

Jack sighed. "Yup, and he's got jurisdiction to investigate federal crimes on the rez."

"With permission," said Dylan.

"Technically. Get ready to be arrested."

Jack parked the SUV and Meadow roused, her words slurred. "We here?"

"Yes, darling," said Dylan.

Jack gave him an odd look and Dylan lifted his chin. Jack's brow quirked in silent question and Dylan nodded.

Yes, this was his woman.

"Okay then," said Jack. "Glad I didn't risk my butt for just anyone."

"I don't expect she'll stay," said Dylan.

Jack looked at Meadow, who rubbed her eyes with both hands. Her wrists were red and raw from the restraints. Her hair stuck up on top like a breaking blue wave and she was still wearing the hospital gown.

"She might surprise you."

Chief Tinnin reached Jack's door. "We have medical. Anyone need a stretcher or wheelchair?"

Jack gave Tinnin a rundown of their injuries as Dylan helped Meadow to a wheelchair. Inside, Dylan refused to leave her as they checked her over and drew blood to determine what they'd given her at the mental-health facility.

Dylan needed his neck wound sutured as he'd torn out several of the staples. Kurt took care of that as Dylan sat at Meadow's side. Late that night, Meadow was moved to a room and Dylan took the bed beside hers. He had planned to keep watch but dozed and woke to someone calling his name. He blinked his eyes open, trying to shake off the grogginess of slumber. Jack stood at the foot of his bed looking worn-out. A glance at the windows showed that morning had come—Monday morning, he realized.

"What time is it?" asked Dylan.

"Nearly nine. I let you sleep as long as I could."

Meadow did not rouse, but her breathing was steady and slow.

Dylan's neck twinged when he sat up, but his throat no longer hurt as much as the soft tissue at his neck. He swung his legs over the side of the narrow hospital bed.

Jack gave him the short version of events.

"We are wanted for the shooting at the facility in Flagstaff. Rhodes's body was not found on the scene. But Crane's was. She's dead."

Dylan knew that meant there was no one to corroborate their version of events.

"Video surveillance?"

"Surprisingly, they have cameras on every corridor. Forrest has a team there."

"They'll see the gunman," said Dylan.

"Maybe."

"You know her mother sent those men. She planned for Meadow to die in there."

"Hard to prove," said Jack. "Her mother is contending that she was worried about Meadow. Her actions come off as those of a concerned parent dealing with a drug-addicted child."

"Meadow doesn't do drugs," said Dylan.

"She's been in detox once after a public indecency charge. She was swimming naked in a fountain at a private country club. According to Forrest her family pulled strings and she got community service."

Dylan realized that no one would believe a thing Meadow said. Not a judge. Not a jury.

"What do we do?"

"You're a war hero. Highly decorated. I'd say your word is good. But Forrest said that the press is spinning you as a PTSD vet with a gun. Morning papers are out. Her mom is good."

"So she's cleared of her husband's murder and she's clear of any charges of wrongdoing regarding Meadow?"

"She will be. I'm certain."

"And we are both wanted?"

Jack nodded. "That's right."

"What does Lupe say about the explosives?"

"She denies any knowledge of her husband's radical involvement."

Dylan swore.

"Oh, and she is suing the papers for mentioning that PAN might be a feeder organization for recruitment to WOLF and BEAR. Forrest says she'll win."

"So she gets away with it all?" asked Dylan.

"The FBI has found nothing to implicate Lupe. But they don't have the explosives, either. Forrest is trying to convince his superiors that the ridge fire was a test and that the real target is one or more of the reservoirs."

"How's that going?" asked Dylan.

Jack shook his head. "Not good."

"If they take out either of the dams above us, it will flood our land."

"Wipe out Piñon Forks completely. Might go as high as Koun'nde."

The two men stared at each other. They both knew they could not let that happen. It was their duty to their people to stop BEAR from destroying their home.

"Skeleton Cliff Dam isn't on our land," said Jack.

"But we have to protect it."

"And Alchesay Canyon," added Jack, naming the dam above Skeleton Cliff and holding back the enormous Goodwin Lake. Below that dam lay Two Mountain Lake, Skeleton Cliff Dam and then their rez, bordering Turquoise Lake. And just beyond their western border was Red Rock Dam, Antelope Lake and, finally, the Mesa Salado Dam. The entire system provided drinking water for both Phoenix and Tucson and supplied the electricity for much of the state. If that was the target, it was a good one. Taking out the dams would send them all back to the 1800s. No air-conditioning, no clean water, no refrigeration. Southwestern Arizona would go from a thriving web of cities to the largest refugee camp in the nation.

Dylan swallowed back the dread at the possibilities. Then he drew a deep breath. The targets were spread over forty of the roughest, most inhospitable miles of territory in the state.

"We need more men," said Dylan.

"Kenshaw is recruiting now. I called my brother Tommy to come home. Kurt is already a full member of Tribal Thunder. Wallace Tinnin wants to move from the Turquoise Guardians to Tribal Thunder, as well. Kenshaw thinks it's a good idea."

The chief of tribal police had always been a leader

of the medicine society, but now he wished to join it to the warrior sect.

"He knows it will be bad," said Dylan.

"We'll need him."

Dylan nodded.

Jack motioned toward Meadow. "She can't go home."

Dylan looked at Meadow's sleeping face and felt a squeezing pressure behind his breastbone.

"I know that. I wanted her to stay because she wanted to, not because she had no other choice."

"You love her?" asked Jack.

Dylan nodded, not taking his eyes off her.

"Always pictured you with an Apache girl."

Dylan looked at Jack.

"Well, sometimes things don't turn out like you plan."

"That's true enough," said Jack.

"You ever going to open that DNA sibling test?" asked Dylan.

"Sometime. Soon maybe."

Dylan knew he'd been carrying the results around with him for weeks.

"Carter would want you to have your answers," said Dylan, certain his twin would not have provided the sample if he objected to Jack discovering the truth.

"What are you going to do?" asked Jack.

"Stay here. Protect the tribe. Protect Meadow. Ask a certain heiress to marry me."

Jack didn't look surprised, rather like he expected Dylan to say something like this.

"Forrest and Cosen won't arrest us on federal land, but they can't keep state officials from trying."

"We have to stay on Indian land."

"For a while."

"Suits me." He wondered how Meadow would do without her parties and clubs and private limo.

"You marry her and she's protected, too," said Jack. "Otherwise, the sheriff can execute a warrant here."

"I don't want her to marry me because she has to."

Jack shrugged. "She doesn't seem the sort not to do what she pleases."

"How will I know?"

"What?"

"If she is marrying me for me or because I can protect her?"

Jack scratched the back of his head. "Don't know."

Dylan moved to stand over Meadow. He stroked her tangled hair from her face.

"I love her, Jack. And I want her to love me back."

Chapter Twenty-Five

Meadow opened her eyes to find herself lying in a twin bed beneath a familiar red, black and turquoise blanket. She fingered the wool and sank down against clean sheets that smelled of bleach and soap. This was Dylan's guest room and library. He had brought her here after the fire.

"You awake now?" The woman's voice was melodious, almost a song.

Meadow opened her eyes to see an unfamiliar Apache woman sitting beside her. The woman lowered the sewing she had on her lap and met Meadow's gaze with directness. There was something very familiar about her.

"My son asked me to watch over you. He is meeting with the FBI and tribal leadership. I'm Dotty Tehauno, Dylan's mom."

Meadow pushed herself up to her elbows and blinked at the woman. The resemblance between mother and son was remarkable, especially around the eyes and mouth, but in Dotty the generous mouth seemed more welcoming and her eyes were more speculative.

"You've been asleep all day. It's Tuesday afternoon now."

Meadow vaguely recalled being lifted from a vehicle and carried through the bright afternoon sunlight. Was that yesterday?

Jack had woken her at the medical clinic and the doctor had checked her over before releasing her. They had wanted her out of there before the sheriff came looking for her and Dylan had driven her here.

The woman offered her a drink and Meadow swallowed one mouthful after another. Apple juice, she realized, sweet and wonderful. The woman helped her set the glass on the side table.

"He's never asked me to watch over a woman before. He said you're important. So what I want to know is if you are important to this investigation or important to my son."

Both, she hoped. "Dylan saved my life."

"More than once, if I can believe Ray Strong, and usually I don't. He just got back from that ridge fire. It's out but burned fifteen thousand acres. Be some mudslides with the rain, I'll bet. Dylan should have been there, too. Fighting that fire. Now he won't get paid." Her expression showed reproach. Both women knew why Dylan was not on the line with his crew.

"I have money," said Meadow.

"No, you don't. You used to have money. Now you've got a crazy mother who wants you dead, a brother who is planning to blow up the parts of the state that they didn't burn down and a father who died trying to save you. I'm sorry to hear about your father. But what you don't have is money. Not anymore.

So that might make you think that you need to find someone who can protect you, because you don't have money to do that anymore. So I wanted to tell you this. My son is not your protector. My son deserves a woman who loves him and who can defend herself."

Meadow felt herself being judged and found lacking. But why not? What had she done with her life but screw up? She tried to think of one redeeming act she had accomplished with her advantages and could not come up with a single thing.

Her head bowed. "I think you're right."

She was met with silence. Meadow looked up to find Dotty regarding her with cautious eyes.

"Your son is a wonderful man. He's smart and brave and selfless. He deserves someone like that."

"But you're not smart?"

"I'm smart. But I didn't do well in school. Schools," she corrected.

"I heard you went to the FBI and told them about your mother."

That made her look like a traitor, Meadow knew, turning in her own mother.

Meadow nodded.

"I think that is brave."

Meadow narrowed her eyes at Dotty. Was she playing some game with her?

Dotty lifted the fabric on her lap and placed another row of careful stitches.

"That leaves selfless." She flicked her gaze from the seam to Meadow. "What are you prepared to sacrifice?"

"I'd give my life for Dylan."

"Very dramatic. Sticking around would be harder. His father left us when he was young. My son has always felt that loss. He needs someone who will stay. If you can't do that, you'd better go sooner rather than later."

"I don't even know if he wants me to stay."

Dotty lifted the stitching. "He asked me to watch over you."

Meadow puzzled over this cryptic reply.

"I need to go find him,"

"No. You need to eat and to bathe." Dotty stood and set her work on the chair. "I'll fix you some lunch. Shower is that way." She pointed toward the door.

"Thank you, Mrs. Tehauno, for your kindness."

Dotty harrumphed and then disappeared down the hall, muttering that she hoped her son had some food in the house.

Meadow showered, working out the kinks and examining the bruises she'd gotten during their escape from the mental hospital.

The water poured down on Meadow's body as she added shampoo to her hair.

Two more people dead and her mother was responsible for it all. No, not her mother. Her father's wife. That meant the siblings who had always looked just a little different than she did shared a father.

So who was her mother? Meadow rinsed the shampoo away. She didn't know who her mother was or what had happened to her, but she intended to find out.

Dylan had told Meadow about his friend Jack. He had suspected most of his life that his father was not the same as his brothers. Why hadn't Meadow ever suspected? Why had she spent most of her life trying to get the only woman she ever knew as her mother to notice her?

To love her.

Meadow let the water wash away her tears along with the soap. Lupe hated her because she was the visible reminder of her husband's love for another woman. An infidelity. A betrayal.

Meadow turned off the taps and reached for a towel. She borrowed Dylan's deodorant and brush, then used the toothbrush he had given her during the first time she'd been here. When she returned to Dylan's spare room it was to find her bed made and a clean set of clothing placed on the blanket.

The jeans were big on her, but the sports bra and underwear fit perfectly. She had fastened the pearl snaps of the green-checked Western-style cotton shirt when she smelled the mouthwatering aroma of fresh-brewed coffee, eggs and sausage. She followed her nose to the kitchen and discovered that Dotty had added fried potatoes to the offering.

"This smells wonderful."

"Everything does when you are hungry." Dotty handed her a plate and motioned to the frying pans. "I made this because it is quick. You eat meat, don't you?"

"Yes, I do," said Meadow as she helped herself to some of everything.

"Fine. You must be starving."

"I'm going to burn that hospital gown," said Meadow.

"I already threw it in the trash," said Dotty.

They shared a smile.

"Thank you for the clothing."

"Those belonged to my youngest daughter, Rita, when she was a teenager. She wore it for barrel racing. I never throw anything out."

"Well, lucky for me," said Meadow, and she settled in at the table before her full plate.

"Eat," said Dotty, and Meadow dug in.

Meadow was on her second helping when Dylan arrived and joined her. Dotty said her goodbyes and left them alone.

Suddenly Meadow felt afraid. She wasn't brave or smart or selfless. She was a trainwreck about to blow the one chance she had with a man whom she loved with every ounce of her being.

The men in her past had been interested in her for the obvious reasons. Sex, of course, but also her money and all that came with it. Dylan wasn't like them. But who was she now that she was not the youngest daughter of Theron and Lupe Wrangler?

"How you feeling?" asked Dylan.

"Clearheaded for a change." *And terrified*, she thought. "Thank you for getting me out of there.

"Why'd you come back for me?" she asked, and then she stilled at the intent look he cast her. She couldn't seem to draw a full breath under the incredulous stare.

"You needed help."

She bowed her head. "Oh, yeah. I really did. You must get tired of pulling my fanny from the fire."

He said nothing.

Meadow glanced up. "I heard Ray Strong is home."

"Safe and sound. He wants to see you, but I held him off."

His friend wanted to check on her. That was good, wasn't it?

"That'd be great."

Dylan grabbed a plate and filled it with eggs and potatoes, then joined her. He polished off the food in short order. When he had finished his meal, he retrieved his coffee mug, cupping it between both his strong hands as he settled across from her once more.

Her belly twitched at the urge she suppressed to stroke those long elegant fingers.

"You spoke with the FBI?" asked Meadow.

"Yes. Forrest and Cosen will want to talk with you again. They have some options for you."

She swallowed and placed a hand over her quaking stomach as she met his gaze across the table. This was bad.

"Options?"

"Yeah. Like you could be relocated as a protected witness."

Meadow felt her heart clench. His friend Carter and his wife, Amber, had entered that program. They had been gone for months and had still not testified in the federal case against the surviving gunman. The thought of being separated from Dylan for such an extended period made her entire body ache. What would she do if he sent her away?

But why would he want her to remain? She'd been trouble for him since the moment they met. That's what she was everywhere she went. Her one true gift was her ability to make a mess.

"I'd rather not," she said.

He exhaled and his hold on the coffee mug tightened. Had he hoped to have someone take her off his hands?

"I can't go home."

"No, you sure can't. Trouble is that Forrest's superiors are not convinced of your mother's involvement. She is contending that she was unaware of her husband's illegal activities."

"What about last night? Rhodes was there to kill me, and my father could not have sent him or the other gunmen."

"She denies any knowledge of why he might have attacked you or of the two men who killed Louisa Crane at the medical health facility. If she's as good as Forrest suspects, there will be nothing to connect any of this to her. She's used your dad as a shield between her and the operation for years. As far as the FBI can determine, Rhodes worked for your father."

"What about the other two?"

"Gone."

"What about the explosives?"

"All I know is what Cosen told me. The traces from the ridge-fire explosion match the type taken from the Lilac mine."

"Did you tell them that the reservoir system is the target?"

"They know. Our word against your mother's, and there is zero evidence she was up there with us that day."

"But the FBI will protect the reservoirs. Right?"

Dylan pressed his lips together. "I hope so. Forrest is worried the bureau might not find the intel credible."

"That's a fancy way to say that they think we made it all up."

He nodded.

"Sure," she said. "Why wouldn't they? I'm crazy. Right? Just broke out of a psych ward. All hopped up on who knows what." Meadow found herself pacing across the kitchen floor.

Dylan stood and captured her in his arms and drew her back so that his mouth was beside her cheek.

"*I* believe you."

She turned toward him, lifting her arms to loop around his neck. How she wanted him. Deep down and with every part of her.

"Our tribal leadership has met with our medicine society. Tribal Thunder will protect the reservoirs."

"All of them?"

Dylan nodded. "Yes, all. Because if any of the dams above our reservation fail, they will take out the next and the next."

How many of his people might die in such a flood?

"Dylan, I don't want to be relocated."

His expression gave away nothing as he continued to stare.

"I want to stay here and guard the reservoirs… with you."

"It's dangerous."

"I know."

"And boring. Guard duty isn't like, well, the life you are used to living."

"I know that, too."

"And it's not your land."

"My mother and father did this. I have a responsibility to set this right."

"Is that why you want to stay? Out of duty?" He leaned forward, as if her answer was important to him.

"Partly."

"What's the other part, Meadow?"

She looked away and realized she was not as brave as Dotty gave her credit for. Not brave enough to say that she loved Dylan, because to say that aloud was to risk her heart. And that was something far more fragile than a life.

"Forrest said that as long as you stay on federal land he can keep the sheriff and highway patrol from getting to you. You won't be arrested or detained. But you are wanted for questioning in the death of your father."

She felt her skin prickle. "They think I killed him?"

"Forrest says they think that Mark Perkinson shot him and that your father shot Perkinson. You and I are witnesses."

"I see."

"Both Forrest and Cosen think your mother might try again. That's why they are recommending witness protection."

"I see." She drew back. His hands brushed her hips as he released her. "I suppose she canceled my credit cards."

"I would. Your father left no will. His estate will go to probate, but…"

"She gets it all."

He nodded.

"It was all hers to begin with." She raked her fingers through her drying hair. "I want to find out about my real mother."

"We can try. There have to be records."

"I need to know who I really am."

Dylan nodded. "Everyone does. But you are who you make yourself. We choose who we will become."

She nodded. There was truth in that. Who did she want to become? Her gaze met his.

"You could stay here with us."

"Your tribe, you mean?"

"With me."

He looked frightened for the first time since she had met him. His fingers drummed on his thighs like a piano player practicing scales, and his entire body looked as tense as one big muscle spasm.

"Dylan, do you want me to stay here with you?" She bit her lower lip as she waited for his reply.

She watched his Adam's apple bob.

"I want you to stay with me, and not because you have to or because you'll be arrested if you leave. I want to know that you…" He pressed his hand to his forehead as if taking his own temperature. Then he blew out a breath.

Hope swelled in that place behind her breastbone, right beside her heart. Dylan wanted her to love him and to stay because there was no other choice but to be where he was—always.

She stepped forward, filled with a hope that he wanted her as much as she wanted him. Meadow took both her hands in his and squeezed.

"Dylan, if I stay it will not be because of the danger of leaving, or because the FBI recommends it, or because you are willing to protect me. It will be because you love me, too."

"Too?" he asked.

She nodded.

He sucked in a breath of surprise and then wrapped her up in his arms so tight she could barely breathe. Then he gripped her shoulders and pushed her back so he could look at her upturned face.

"You love me?" he asked.

"I do. So much that the thought of leaving you hurts. I need to be with you and I'll help you fight them."

"I was afraid you'd have no choice. Marrying me would give you the protection of a full member of the tribe."

"And you thought I'd do that to save my own skin."

He lowered his head until his forehead pressed to hers. "I just wanted you to have a choice."

"I do have a choice."

"And you'll marry me?" he asked.

She stepped back. "No."

His smile fell away.

"No?" he asked.

"No. I won't. I'll stay here and fight with you. I'll love you until you have no doubt, and when we have stopped them and I'm free, then I'll marry you."

"We don't have to wait."

"Yes, we do. Not just for you, Dylan. For me, too. I want everyone to know why I choose you. I won't have your tribe thinking you married me from pity or that I had to be your bride. I won't marry you— because I love you too much."

Dylan smiled and then he nodded. "Once they know you, they'll know why you stay."

She was giving him what he needed. Dylan would keep his dignity and she would find pride in doing something of use.

"This will be a new experience for me," she said. "I'm more the immediate-gratification kind of gal."

"Patience comes with its own reward." There was a certain twinkle in his eyes that made her blood rush.

"Oh, yeah?"

He looped an arm around her shoulder and leaned in, taking the lobe of her ear into his mouth. Tiny ripples of pleasure cascaded along every nerve, and she trembled with anticipation.

Dylan drew back and looked down at her, his smile wicked.

"Withholding personal gratification makes the pleasure more satisfying," he said.

"I'm looking forward to trying that sometime," she said as she steered him down the hall toward his bedroom. "But not today."

She thought about the first time she'd laid eyes on him, when she'd blocked his way up that ridge, delaying him just enough that he had survived the blast, and then he'd rescued her.

It was important that he know her heart, and it would take time to show him—and his people—that this outsider had changed her ways and was here for the duration.

They were a team and they were in love. She didn't need a wedding band as evidence of his devotion. His mouth and his hands and his heart were proof enough.

She knew the July monsoons were coming. Knew, too, that the reservoirs would be full to bursting after the storms. This would be the time to strike, when the damage would be most great.

Meadow knew all that, and she knew that they must stop her mother and the extremists of BEAR because Meadow and the brave warriors of Tribal Thunder would protect what they loved.

Meadow's heart beat with hope and excitement. She was no longer lost or alone because she had found her place and her purpose. Dylan had given her so much more than his love. He had given her respect, a mission larger than herself and a chance to make a difference in the world. She felt ready for what would come; ready to join Dylan in this fight and ready to become the woman worthy of his love.

Bobcat had found a mate.

"You are my heartbeat," she said and kissed him long and slow.

* * * * *

Prepare as tribal police detective Jack Bear Den goes undercover with FBI field agent Sophia Fowler in the final showdown between the eco-extremists of BEAR and the warriors of Tribal Thunder in book 4, TURQUOISE WARRIORS, coming June 2017.

SPECIAL EXCERPT FROM

⊞ HARLEQUIN®

I N T R I G U E

*Detective Ronan Cavanaugh O'Bannon will do
whatever it takes to protect one of the Cavanaughs' own
from a serial killer sweeping through Aurora, including
working with wild-card detective Sierra Carlyle.*

Read on for a sneak preview of
CAVANAUGH STANDOFF,
the next book in USA TODAY *bestselling author*
Marie Ferrarella's fan-favorite series
CAVANAUGH JUSTICE.

He knew he had to utilize her somehow, and maybe
she could be useful. "All right, you might as well come
along. You might come in handy if there's a next of kin
to notify." Ronan began walking back to his car. "I'm not
much good at that."

"I'm surprised," Sierra commented.

Reaching the car, Ronan turned to look at her. "If
you're going to be sarcastic—"

"No, I'm serious," she told him, then went on to
explain her rationale. "You're so detached, I just assumed
it wouldn't bother you to tell a person that someone
they'd expected to come home was never going to do that
again. It would bother them, of course," she couldn't help
adding, "but not you."

Ronan got into his vehicle, buckled up and pulled
out in what seemed like one fluid motion, all the while

chewing on what this latest addition to his team had just said. Part of him just wanted to let it go. But he couldn't.

"I'm not heartless," he informed her. "I just don't allow emotions to get in the way and I don't believe in using more words than are absolutely necessary," he added pointedly since he knew that seemed to bother her.

"Well, lucky for you, I do," she told him with what amounted to the beginnings of a smile. "I guess that's what'll make us such good partners."

He looked at her, stunned. He viewed them as being like oil and water—never able to mix. "Is that your take on this?" he asked incredulously.

"Yes," she answered cheerfully.

The fact that she appeared to have what one of his brothers would label a "killer smile" notwithstanding, Ronan just shook his head. "Unbelievable."

"Oh, you'll get to believe it soon enough," she told him. Before he could say anything, Sierra just continued talking to him and got down to the immediate business at hand. "I'm going to need to see your files on the other murders once we're back in the squad room so I can be brought up to date."

He didn't even spare her a look. "Fine."

"Are you always this cheerful?" she asked. "Or is there something in particular that's bothering you?"

Don't miss
CAVANAUGH STANDOFF by Marie Ferrarella,
available June 2017 wherever
Harlequin® Intrigue books and ebooks are sold.

www.Harlequin.com

JUST CAN'T GET ENOUGH?

Join our social communities
and talk to us online.

You will have access to the latest
news on upcoming titles and special
promotions, but most importantly,
you can talk to other fans about your
favorite Harlequin reads.

Harlequin.com/Community

Facebook.com/HarlequinBooks

Twitter.com/HarlequinBooks

Pinterest.com/HarlequinBooks

THE WORLD IS BETTER WITH

Romance

Harlequin has everything from contemporary, passionate and heartwarming to suspenseful and inspirational stories.

Whatever your mood,
we have a romance just for you!

Love the Harlequin book
you just read?

Your opinion matters.

Review this book on your favorite
book site, review site, blog or your own
social media properties and share
your opinion with other readers!

Be sure to connect with us at:
Harlequin.com/Newsletters
Facebook.com/HarlequinBooks
Twitter.com/HarlequinBooks